Classic Espionage Stories

Classic Espionage Stories
from a
Suitcase of Suspense

The Reader's Digest Association, Inc.
Pleasantville, New York•Montreal

MQ PUBLICATIONS PROJECT STAFF
Project Editor: Nicola Birtwisle
Project Designer: Jason Anscomb

READER'S DIGEST PROJECT STAFF
Project Editor: Nancy Shuker
Project Designer: George McKeon

READER'S DIGEST BOOKS
Editor-in-Chief: Christopher Cavanagh
Executive Editor, Trade Publishing: Dolores York
Senior Design Director: Elizabeth Tunnicliffe
Director, Trade Publishing: Christopher T. Reggio

Library of Congress Cataloging-in-Publication Data

Classic espionage stories from a suitcase of suspense.
    p. cm.
    Contents: The rocking-horse spy / by Ted Allbeury – The brass butterfly / by William
Le Queux – Match point in Berlin / by Patricia McGerr – The Bruce-Partington plans /
by Arthur Conan Doyle – The interrogation of the prisoner Bung by Mister Hawkins and
Sergeant Tree / by David Huddle – The purloined letter / by Edgar Allan Poe.
    ISBN 0-7621-0373-6
    1. Spy stories, American. 2. Spy stories, English. I. Title: Suitcase of suspense.

PS648.S85 C43 2002
813'.087208–dc21

                                                        2001048630

Address any comments about SUITCASE OF SUSPENSE to:
        The Reader's Digest Association, Inc.
        Adult Trade Publishing
        Reader's Digest Road
        Pleasantville, NY 10570-7000

For more Reader's Digest
products and information,
visit our online store at

rd.com

Printed and bound in China

3 5 7 9 10 8 6 4 2

CONTENTS

THE PURLOINED LETTER

BY EDGAR ALLAN POE

Nil sapientiæ odiosius acumine nimio.
—Seneca

At Paris, just after dark one gusty evening in the autumn of 18—, I was enjoying the twofold luxury of meditation and a meerschaum, in company with my friend C. Auguste Dupin, in his little back library, or book-closet, *au troisème, No. 33, Rue Dunôt, Faubourg St. Germain.* For one hour at least we had maintained a profound silence; while each, to any casual observer, might have seemed intently and exclusively occupied with the curling eddies of smoke that oppressed the atmosphere of the chamber. For myself, however, I was mentally discussing certain topics which had formed matter for conversation between us at an earlier period of the evening; I mean the affair of the Rue Morgue, and the mystery attending the murder of Marie Rogêt. I looked upon it, therefore, as something of a coincidence, when the door of our apartment was thrown open and admitted our old acquaintance, Monsieur G—, the Prefect of the Parisian police.

We gave him a hearty welcome; for there was nearly half as much of the entertaining as of the contemptible about the man, and we had not seen him for several years. We had been sitting in the dark, and Dupin now arose for the purpose of lighting a lamp, but sat down again, without doing so, upon G—'s saying that he had called to consult us, or rather to ask the opinion of my friend, about some official business which had occasioned a great deal of trouble.

"If it is any point requiring reflection," observed Dupin, as he forbore to enkindle the wick, "we shall examine it to better purpose in the dark."

"That is another of your odd notions," said the Prefect, who had a fashion of calling everything "odd" that was beyond his comprehension, and thus lived amid an absolute legion of "oddities."

"Very true," said Dupin, as he supplied his visitor with a pipe, and rolled towards him a comfortable chair.

"And what is the difficulty now?" I asked. "Nothing more in the assassination way, I hope?"

"Oh no; nothing of that nature. The fact is, the business is very simple indeed, and I make no doubt that we can manage it sufficiently well ourselves; but then I thought Dupin would like to hear the details of it, because it is so excessively *odd*."

"Simple and odd," said Dupin.

"Why, yes; and not exactly that, either. The fact is, we have all been a good deal puzzled because the affair *is* so simple, and yet baffles us altogether."

"Perhaps it is the very simplicity of the thing which puts you at fault," said my friend.

"What nonsense you *do* talk!" replied the Prefect, laughing heartily.

"Perhaps the mystery is a little *too* plain," said Dupin.

"Oh, good heavens! Who ever heard of such an idea?"

"A little *too* self-evident."

"Ha! ha! ha!—ha! ha! ha!-ho! ho! ho!"—roared our visitor, profoundly amused, "oh Dupin, you will be the death of me yet!"

"And what, after all, *is* the matter on hand?" I asked.

"Why, I will tell you," replied the Prefect, as he gave a long, steady, and contemplative puff, and settled himself in his chair. "I will tell you in a few words; but, before I begin, let me caution you that this is an affair demanding the greatest secrecy, and that I should most probably lose the position I now hold, were it known that I confided it to any one."

"Proceed," said I.

"Or not," said Dupin.

"Well, then; I have received personal information, from a very high quarter, that a certain document of the last importance, has been purloined from the royal apartments. The individual who purloined it is known; this beyond a doubt; he was seen to take it. It is known, also, that it still remains in his possession."

"How is this known?" asked Dupin.

"It is clearly inferred," replied the Prefect, "from the nature of the document, and from the non-appearance of certain results which would at once arise from its passing *out* of the robber's possession;—that is to say, from his employing it as he must design in the end to employ it."

"Be a little more explicit," I said.

"Well, I may venture so far as to say that the paper gives its holder a certain power in a certain quarter where such power is immensely valuable." The Prefect was fond of the cant of diplomacy.

"Still I do not quite understand," said Dupin.

"No? Well; the disclosure of the document to a third person, who shall be nameless, would bring in question the honour of a personage of most exalted station; and this fact gives the holder of the document an ascendancy over the illustrious personage whose honour and peace are so jeopardised."

"But this ascendancy," I interposed, "would depend upon the robber's knowledge of the loser's knowledge of the robber. Who would dare—"

"The thief," said G—, "is the Minister D—, who dares all things, those unbecoming as well as those becoming a man. The method of the theft was not less ingenious than bold. The document in question—a letter, to be frank—had been received by the personage robbed while alone in the royal *boudoir*. During its perusal she was suddenly interrupted by the entrance of the other exalted personage from whom especially it was her wish to conceal it. After a hurried and vain endeavour to thrust it in a drawer, she was forced to place it, open as it was, upon a table. The address, however, was uppermost, and the contents thus unexposed, the letter escaped notice. At this juncture enters the Minister D—. His lynx eye immediately perceives the paper, recognises the handwriting of the address, observes the confusion of the personage addressed, and fathoms her secret. After some business transactions, hurried through in his ordinary manner, he produces a letter somewhat similar to the one in question, opens it, pretends to read it, and then places it in close juxtaposition to the other. Again he converses, for some fifteen minutes, upon the public affairs. At length, in taking leave, he takes also from the table the letter to which he had no claim. Its rightful owner saw, but, of course, dared not call attention to the act, in the presence of the third personage who stood at her elbow. The minister decamped; leaving his own letter—one of no importance—upon the table."

"Here, then," said Dupin to me, "you have precisely what you demand to make the ascendancy complete—the robber's knowledge of the loser's knowledge of the robber."

"Yes," replied the Prefect; "and the power thus attained has, for some months past, been wielded, for political purposes, to a very dangerous extent. The personage robbed is more thoroughly convinced, every day, of the necessity of reclaiming her letter. But this, of course, cannot be done openly. In fine, driven to despair, she has committed the matter to me."

"Than whom," said Dupin, amid a perfect whirlwind of smoke, "no more sagacious agent could, I suppose, be desired, or even imagined."

"You flatter me," replied the Prefect; "but it is possible that some such opinion may have been entertained."

"It is clear," said I, "as you observe, that the letter is still in possession of the minister; since it is this possession, and not any employment of the letter, which bestows the power. With the employment the power departs."

"True," said G—; "and upon this conviction I proceeded. My first care was to make thorough search of the minister's hotel; and here my chief embarrassment lay in the necessity of searching without his knowledge. Beyond all things, I have been warned of the danger which would result from giving him reason to suspect our design."

"But," said I, "you are quite *au fait* in these investigations. The Parisian police have done this thing often before."

"Oh yes; and for this reason I did not despair. The habits of the minister gave me, too, a great advantage. He is frequently absent from home all night. His servants are by no means numerous. They sleep at a distance from their master's apartment, and, being chiefly Neapolitans, are readily made drunk. I have keys, as you know, with which I can open any chamber or cabinet in Paris. For three months a night has not passed, during the greater part of which I have not been engaged, personally, in ransacking the D— hotel. My honour is interested, and, to mention a great secret, the reward is enormous. So I did not abandon the search until I had become fully satisfied that the thief is a more astute man than myself. I fancy that I have investigated every nook and corner of the premises in which it is possible that the paper can be concealed."

"But is it not possible," I suggested, "that although the letter may be in the possession of the minister, as it unquestionably is, he may have concealed it elsewhere than upon his own premises?"

"This is barely possible," said Dupin. "The present peculiar condition of affairs at court, and especially of those intrigues in which D— is known to be involved, would render the instant availability of the document—its susceptibility of being produced at a moment's notice—a point of nearly equal importance with its possession."

"Its susceptibility of being produced?" said I.

"That is to say, of being *destroyed*," said Dupin.

"True," I observed; "the paper is clearly then upon the premises. As for its being upon the person of the minister, we may consider that as out of the question."

"Entirely," said the Prefect. "He has been twice waylaid, as if by footpads, and his person rigorously searched under my own inspection."

"You might have spared yourself this trouble," said Dupin. "D——, I presume, is not altogether a fool, and, if not, must have anticipated these waylayings, as a matter of course."

"Not *altogether* a fool," said G——, "but then he's a poet, which I take to be only one remove from a fool."

"True," said Dupin, after a long and thoughtful whiff from his meerschaum, "although I have been guilty of certain doggerel myself."

"Suppose you detail," said I, "the particulars of your search."

"Why, the fact is, we took our time, and we searched *everywhere*. I have had long experience in these affairs. I took the entire building, room by room; devoting the nights of a whole week to each. We examined, first, the furniture of each apartment. We opened every possible drawer; and I presume you know that to a properly trained police agent, such a thing as a *secret* drawer is impossible. Any man is a dolt who permits a "secret" drawer to escape him in a search of this kind. The thing is *so* plain. There is a certain amount of bulk—of space—to be accounted for in every cabinet. Then we have accurate rules. The fiftieth part of a line could not escape us. After the cabinets we took the chairs. The cushions we probed with the fine long needles you have seen me employ. From the tables we removed the tops."

"Why so?"

"Sometimes the top of a table, or other similarly arranged piece of furniture, is removed by the person wishing to conceal an article; then the leg is excavated, the article deposited within the cavity, and the top replaced. The bottoms and tops of bedposts are employed in the same way."

"But could not the cavity be detected by sounding?" I asked.

"By no means, if, when the article is deposited, a sufficient wadding of cotton be placed around it. Besides, in our case, we were obliged to proceed without noise."

"But you could not have removed—you could not have taken to pieces *all* articles of furniture in which it would have been possible to make a deposit in the manner you mention. A letter may be compressed into a thin spiral roll, not differing much in shape or bulk from a large knitting-needle, and in this form it might be inserted into the rung of a chair, for example. You did not take to pieces all the chairs?"

"Certainly not; but we did better—we examined the rungs of every chair in the hotel, and, indeed, the jointings of every description of furniture, by the aid of a most powerful microscope. Had there been any traces of recent disturbance we should not have failed to detect it instantly. A single grain of gimlet-dust, for example, would have been as obvious as an apple. Any disorder in the glueing—any unusual gaping in the joints—would have sufficed to insure detection."

"I presume you looked to the mirrors, between the boards and the plates, and you probed the beds and the bed-clothes, as well as the curtains and carpets."

"That of course; and when we had absolutely completed every particle of the furniture in this way, then we examined the house itself. We divided its entire surface into compartments, which we numbered, so that none might be missed; then we scrutinised each individual square inch throughout the premises, including the two houses immediately adjoining, with the microscope, as before."

"The two houses adjoining!" I exclaimed; "you must have had a great deal of trouble."

"We had; but the reward offered is prodigious."

"You include the *grounds* about the houses?"

"All the grounds are paved with brick. They gave us comparatively little trouble. We examined the moss between the bricks, and found it undisturbed."

"You looked among D—'s papers, of course, and into the books of the library?"

"Certainly; we opened every package and parcel; we not only opened every book, but we turned over every leaf in each volume, not contenting ourselves with a mere shake, according to the fashion of some of our police officers. We also measured the thickness of every book-*cover*, with the most accurate admeasurement, and applied to each the most jealous scrutiny of the microscope. Had any of the bindings been recently meddled with, it would have been utterly impossible that the fact should have escaped observation. Some five or six volumes, just from the hands of the binder, we carefully probed, longitudinally, with the needles."

"You explored the floors beneath the carpets?"

"Beyond doubt. We removed every carpet, and examined the boards with the microscope."

"And the paper on the walls?"

"Yes."

"You looked into the cellars?"

"We did."

"Then," I said, "you have been making a miscalculation, and the letter is *not* upon the premises, as you suppose."

"I fear you are right there," said the Prefect. "And now, Dupin, what would you advise me to do?"

"To make a thorough re-search of the premises."

"That is absolutely needless," replied G—. "I am not more sure that I breathe than I am that the letter is not at the hotel."

"I have no better advice to give you," said Dupin. "You have, of course, an accurate description of the letter?"

"Oh yes!"—And here the Prefect, producing a memorandum book, proceeded to read aloud a minute account of the internal, and especially of the external appearance of the missing document. Soon after finishing the perusal of this description, he took his departure, more entirely depressed in spirits than I had ever known the good gentleman before.

In about a month afterwards he paid us another visit, and found us occupied very nearly as before. He took a pipe and a chair and entered into some ordinary conversation. At length I said—

"Well, but G—, what of the purloined letter? I presume you have at last made up your mind that there is no such thing as overreaching the minister?"

"Confound him, say I—yes; I made the re-examination, however, as Dupin suggested—but it was all labour lost, as I knew it would be."

"How much was the reward offered, did you say?" asked Dupin.

"Why, a very great deal—a *very* liberal reward—I don't like to say how much, precisely; but one thing I *will* say, that I wouldn't mind giving my individual check for fifty thousand francs to anyone who could obtain me that letter. The fact is, it is becoming of more and more importance every day; and the reward has been lately doubled. If it were trebled, however, I could do no more than I have done."

"Why, yes," said Dupin, drawlingly, between the whiffs of his meerschaum, "I really—think, G—, you have not exerted yourself—to the utmost in this matter. You might—do a little more, I think, eh?"

"How?—in what way?"

"Why—puff, puff—you might—puff, puff—employ counsel in the matter, eh?—puff, puff, puff. Do you remember the story they tell of Abernethy?"

"No; hang Abernethy!"

"To be sure! hang him and welcome. But, once upon a time, a certain rich miser conceived the design of spunging upon this Abernethy for a medical opinion. Getting up, for this purpose, an ordinary conversation in a private company, he insinuated his case to the physician as that of an imaginary individual.

" 'We will suppose,' said the miser, 'that his symptoms are such and such; now, doctor, what would *you* have directed him to take?' "

"'Take!' said Abernethy, 'why, take *advice*, to be sure.'"

"But," said the Prefect, a little discomposed, "I am *perfectly* willing to take advice, and to pay for it. I would *really* give fifty thousand francs to any one who would aid me in the matter."

"In that case," replied Dupin, opening a drawer, and producing a check-book, "you may as well fill me up a check for the amount mentioned. When you have signed it, I will hand you the letter."

I was astounded. The Prefect appeared absolutely thunderstricken. For some minutes he remained speechless and motionless, looking incredulously at my friend with open mouth, and eyes that seemed starting from their sockets; then, apparently recovering himself in some measure, he seized a pen, and after several pauses and vacant stares, finally filled up and signed a check for fifty thousand francs, and handed it across the table to Dupin. The latter examined it carefully and deposited it in his pocket-book; then, unlocking an *escritoire*, took thence a letter and gave it to the Prefect. This functionary grasped it in a perfect agony of joy, opened it with a trembling hand, cast a rapid glance at its contents, and then, scrambling and struggling to the door, rushed at length unceremoniously from the room and from the house, without having uttered a syllable since Dupin had requested him to fill up the check.

When he had gone, my friend entered into some explanations.

"The Parisian police," he said, "are exceedingly able in their way. They are persevering, ingenious, cunning, and thoroughly versed in the knowledge which their duties seem chiefly to demand. Thus, when G— detailed to us his mode of searching the premises at the Hôtel D—, I felt entire confidence in his having made a satisfactory investigation—so far as his labours extended."

"So far as his labours extended?" said I.

"Yes," said Dupin. "The measures adopted were not only the best of their kind, but carried out to absolute perfection. Had the letter been deposited within the range of their search, these fellows would, beyond a question, have found it."

I merely laughed—but he seemed quite serious in all that he said.

"The measures, then," he continued, "were good in their kind, and well executed; their defect lay in their being inapplicable to the case, and to the man. A certain set of highly ingenious resources are, with the Prefect, a sort of Procrustean bed, to which he forcibly adapts his designs. But he perpetually errs by being too deep or too shallow for the matter in hand; and many a schoolboy is a better reasoner than he. I knew one about eight years of age whose success at guessing in the game of 'even and odd' attracted universal admiration. This game is simple, and played with marbles. One player holds in his hand a number of these toys, and demands of another whether that number is even or odd. If the guess is right, the guesser wins one; if wrong, he loses one. The boy to whom I allude won all the marbles of the school. Of course he had some principle of guessing; and this lay in mere observation and admeasurement of the astuteness of his opponents. For example, an arrant simpleton is his opponent, and, holding up his closed hand, asks, 'Are they even or odd?' Our schoolboy replies, 'odd,' and loses; but upon the second trial he wins, for he then says to himself, 'the simpleton had them even upon the first trial, and his amount of cunning is just sufficient to make him have them odd upon the second; I will therefore guess odd';—he guesses odd, and wins. Now, with a simpleton a degree above the first, he would have reasoned thus: 'This fellow finds that in the first instance I guessed odd, and, in the second, he will propose to himself upon the first impulse, a simple variation from even to odd, as did the first simpleton; but then a second thought will suggest that this is too simple a variation, and finally he will decide upon putting it even as before. I will therefore guess even';—he guesses even, and wins. Now this mode of reasoning in the schoolboy, whom his fellows termed 'lucky',—what, in its last analysis, is it?"

"It is merely," I said, "an identification of the reasoner's intellect with that of his opponent."

"It is," said Dupin; "and, upon inquiring of the boy by what means he effected the *thorough* identification in which his success consisted, I received answer as follows: 'When I wish to find out how wise, or stupid, or how good, or how wicked is any one, or what are his thoughts at the moment, I fashion the expression of my face, as accurately as possible, in accordance with the expression of his, and then wait to see what thoughts of sentiments arise in my mind or heart, as if to match or correspond with the expression.' This response of the schoolboy lies at the bottom of all the spurious profundity which has been attributed to Rochefoucauld, to La Bougive, to Machiavelli, and to Campanella."

"And the identification," I said, "of the reasoner's intellect with that of his opponent, depends, if I understand you aright, upon the accuracy with which the opponent's intellect is admeasured."

"For its practical value it depends upon this," replied Dupin; "and the Prefect and his cohort fail so frequently, first, by default of this identification, and, secondly, by ill-admeasurement, or rather through non-admeasurement, of the intellect with which they are engaged. They consider only their *own* ideas of ingenuity; and, in searching for anything hidden, advert only to the modes in which *they* would have hidden it. They are right in this much—that their own ingenuity is a faithful representative of that of *the mass;* but when the cunning of the individual felon is diverse in character from their own, the felon foils them, of course. This always happens when it is above their own, and very usually when it is below. They have no variation of principle in their investigations; at best, when urged by some unusual emergency—by some extraordinary reward—they extend or exaggerate their old modes of *practice,* without touching their principles. What, for example, in this case of D—, has been done to vary the principle of action? What is all this boring, and probing, and sounding, and scrutinising with the microscope, and dividing the surface of the building into registered square inches—what is it all but an exaggeration *of the application* of the one principle or set of principles of search, which are based upon the one set of notions regarding human ingenuity, to which the Prefect, in the long routine of his duty, has been accustomed? Do you not see he has taken it for granted that *all* men proceed to conceal a letter,—not exactly in a gimlet-hole bored in a chair-leg—but, at least, in *some* out-of-the-way hole or corner suggested by the same tenor of thought which would urge a man to secrete a letter in a gimlet-hole bored in a chair-leg? And do you not see also, that such *recherchés* nooks for concealment are adapted only for ordinary occasions, and would be adopted only by ordinary intellects; for, in all cases of concealment, a disposal of the article concerned—a disposal of it in this *recherché* manner,—is, in the very first instance, presumable and presumed; and thus its discovery depends, not at all upon the acumen, but altogether upon the mere care, patience, and determination of the seekers; and where the case is of importance—or, what amounts to the same thing in the policial eyes, when the reward is of magnitude,—the qualities in question have *never* been known to fail. You will now understand what I mean in suggesting that, had the purloined letter been hidden anywhere within the limits of the Prefect's examination—in other words, had the principle of its concealment been comprehended within the principles of the Prefect—its discovery would have been a matter altogether beyond question. This functionary, however, has been thoroughly mystified; and the remote source of his defeat lies in the supposition that the minister is a fool, because he has acquired renown as a poet. All fools are poets; this the Prefect *feels*; and he is merely guilty of a *non distributio medii* in thence inferring that all poets are fools."

"But is this really the poet?" I asked. "There are two brothers, I know; and both have attained reputation in letters. The minister I believe has written learnedly on the Differential Calculus. He is a mathematician, and no poet."

"You are mistaken; I know him well; he is both. As poet *and* mathematician, he would reason well; as mere mathematician, he could not have reasoned at all, and thus would have been at the mercy of the Prefect."

"You surprise me," I said, "by these opinions, which have been contradicted by the voice of the world. You do not mean to set at naught the well-digested idea of centuries. The mathematical reason has long been regarded as the reason *par excellence*."

" '*Il y a à parier*,' " replied Dupin, quoting from Chamfort, " '*que toute idée publique, toute convention reçue, est une sottise, car elle a convenu au plus grand nombre.*' The mathematicians, I grant you, have done their best to promulgate the popular error to which you allude, and which is none the less an error for its promulgation as truth. With an art worthy a better cause, for example, they have insinuated the term 'analysis' into application to algebra. The French are the originators of this particular deception; but if a term is of any importance—if words derive any value from applicability—then 'analysis' conveys 'algebra' about as much as, in Latin, '*ambitus*' implies 'ambition', '*religio*' 'religion', or '*homines honesti*', a set of *honourable* men."

"You have a quarrel on hand, I see," said I, "with some of the algebraists of Paris; but proceed."

"I dispute the availability, and thus the value, of that reason which is cultivated in any special form other than the abstractly logical. I dispute, in particular, the reason educed by mathematical study. The mathematics are the science of form and quantity; mathematical reasoning is merely logic applied to observation upon form and quantity. The great error lies in supposing that even the truths of what is called *pure* algebra, are abstract or general truths. And this error is so egregious that I am confounded at the universality with which it has been received. Mathematical axioms are *not* axioms of general truth. What is true of *relation*—of form and quantity—is often grossly false in regard to morals, for example. In this latter science it is very usually *un*true that the aggregated parts are equal to the whole. In chemistry also the axiom fails. In the consideration of motive it fails; for two motives, each of a given value, have not, necessarily, a value when united, equal to the sum of their values apart. There are numerous other mathematical truths which are only truths within the limits of *relation*. But the mathematician argues, from his *finite truths,* through habit, as if they were of an absolutely general applicability—as the world indeed imagines them to be. Bryant, in his very learned *Mythology,* mentions an analogous source of error, when he says that 'although the Pagan fables are not believed, yet we forget ourselves continually, and make inferences from them as existing realities.' With the algebraists, however, who are Pagans themselves, the 'Pagan fables' *are* believed, and the inferences are made, not so much through lapse of memory, as through an unaccountable addling of the brains. In short, I never yet encountered the mere mathematician who could be trusted out of equal roots, or one who did not clandestinely hold it as a point of his faith that x^2+px was absolutely and unconditionally equal to q. Say to one of these gentlemen, by way of experiment, if you please, that you believe occasions may occur where x^2+px is *not* altogether equal to q, and, having made him understand what you mean, get out of his reach as speedily as convenient, for, beyond doubt, he will endeavour to knock you down.

"I mean to say," continued Dupin, while I merely laughed at his last observations, "that if the minister had been no more than a mathematician, the Prefect would have been under no necessity of giving me this check. I knew him, however, as both mathematician and poet, and my measures were adapted to his capacity, with reference to the circumstances by which he was surrounded. I knew him as a courtier, too, and as a bold *intrigant*. Such a man, I considered, could not fail to be aware of the ordinary policial modes of action. He could not have failed to anticipate—and events have proved that he did not fail to anticipate—the waylayings to which he was subjected. He must have foreseen, I reflected, the secret investigations of his premises. His frequent absences from home at night, which were hailed by the Prefect as certain aids to his success, I regarded only as *ruses,* to afford opportunity for thorough search to the police, and thus the sooner to impress them with the conviction to which G—, in fact, did finally arrive—the conviction that the letter was not upon the premises. I felt, also, that the whole train of thought, which I was at some pains in detailing to you just now, concerning the invariable principle of policial action in searches for articles concealed—I felt that this whole train of thought would necessarily pass through the mind of the minister. It would imperatively lead him to despise all the ordinary *nooks* of concealment. *He* could not, I reflected, be so weak as not to see that the most intricate and remote recess of his hotel would be as open as his commonest closets to the eyes, to the probes, to the gimlets, and to the microscopes of the Prefect. I saw, in fine, that he would be driven, as a matter of course, to *simplicity,* if not deliberately induced to it as a matter of choice. You will remember, perhaps, how desperately the Prefect laughed when I suggested, upon our first interview, that it was just possible this mystery troubled him so much on account of its being so *very* self-evident."

"Yes," said I, "I remember his merriment well. I really thought he would have fallen into convulsions."

"The material world," continued Dupin, "abounds with very strict analogies to the immaterial; and thus some colour of truth has been given to the rhetorical dogma, that metaphor, or simile, may be made to strengthen an argument, as well as to embellish a description. The principle of the *vis inertiæ,* for example, seems to be identical in physics and metaphysics. It is not more true in the former, that a large body is with more difficulty set in motion than a smaller one, and that its subsequent *momentum* is commensurate with this difficulty, than it is, in the latter, that intellects of the vaster capacity, while more forcible, more constant, and more eventful in their movements than those of inferior grade, are yet the less readily moved, and more embarrassed and full of hesitation in the first few steps of their progress. Again: have you ever noticed which of the street signs, over the shop doors, are the most attractive of attention?"

"I have never given the matter a thought," I said.

"There is a game of puzzles," he resumed, "which is played upon a map. One party playing requires another to find a given word—the name of town, river, state, or empire—any word, in short, upon the motley and perplexed surface of the chart. A novice in the game generally seeks to embarrass his opponents by giving them the most minutely-lettered names; but the adept selects such words as stretch, in large characters, from one end of the chart to the other. These, like the over-largely lettered signs and placards of the street, escape observation by dint of being excessively obvious; and here the physical oversight is precisely analogous with the moral inapprehension by which the intellect suffers to pass unnoticed those considerations which are too obtrusively and too palpably self-evident. But this is a point, it appears, somewhat above or beneath the understanding of the Prefect. He never once thought it probable, or possible, that the minister had deposited the letter immediately beneath the nose of the whole world, by way of best preventing any portion of that world from perceiving it.

"But the more I reflected upon the daring, dashing, and discriminating ingenuity of D—; upon the fact that the document must always have been *at hand,* if he intended to use it to good purpose; and upon the decisive evidence, obtained by the Prefect, that it was not hidden within the limits of that dignitary's ordinary search—the more satisfied I became that, to conceal this letter, the minister had resorted to the comprehensive and sagacious expedient of not attempting to conceal it at all.

"Full of these ideas, I prepared myself with a pair of green spectacles, and called one fine morning quite by accident, at the ministerial hotel. I found D— at home, yawning, lounging, and dawdling, as usual, and pretending to be in the last extremity of *ennui*. He is, perhaps, the most really energetic human being now alive—but that is only when nobody sees him.

"To be even with him, I complained of my weak eyes, and lamented the necessity of the spectacles, under cover of which I cautiously and thoroughly surveyed the apartment, while seemingly intent only upon the conversation of my host.

"I paid special attention to a large writing-table near which he sat, and upon which lay confusedly, some miscellaneous letters and other papers, with one or two musical instruments and a few books. Here, however, after a long and very deliberate scrutiny, I saw nothing to excite particular suspicion.

"At length my eyes, in going the circuit of the room, fell upon a trumpery filigree card-rack of paste-board, that hung dangling by a dirty blue ribbon, from a little brass knob just beneath the middle of the mantel-piece. In this rack, which had three or four compartments, were five or six visiting cards and a solitary letter. This last was much soiled and crumpled. It was torn nearly in two, across the middle—as if a design, in the first instance, to tear it entirely up as worthless, had been altered, or stayed, in the second. It had a large black seal, bearing the D— cipher *very* conspicuously, and was addressed, in a diminutive female hand, to D—, the minister, himself. It was thrust carelessly, and even, as it seemed, contemptuously, into one of the upper divisions of the rack.

"No sooner had I glanced at this letter, that I concluded it to be that of which I was in search. To be sure, it was, to all appearance, radically different from the one of which the Prefect had read us so minute a description. Here the seal was large and black, with the D— cipher; there it was small and red, with the ducal arms of the S— family. Here, the address, to the minister, was diminutive and feminine; there the super-scription, to a certain royal personage, was markedly bold and decided; the size alone formed a point of correspondence. But, then, the *radicalness* of these differences, which was excessive; the dirt; the soiled and torn condition of the paper, so incon-sistent with the *true* methodical habits of D—, and so sugges-tive of a design to delude the beholder into an idea of the worthlessness of the document; these things, together with the hyperobtrusive situation of this document, full in the view of every visitor, and thus exactly in accordance with the conclu-sions to which I had previously arrived; these things, I say, were strongly corroborative of suspicion, in one who came with the intention to suspect.

"I protracted my visit as long as possible, and, while I main-tained a most animated discussion with the minister, on a topic which I knew well had never failed to interest and excite him, I kept my attention really riveted upon the letter. In this examina-tion, I committed to memory its external appearance and arrange-ment in the rack; and also fell, at length, upon a discovery which set at rest whatever trivial doubt I might have entertained. In scru-tinising the edges of the paper, I observed them to be more *chafed* than seemed necessary. They presented the *broken* appearance which is manifested when a stiff paper, having been once folded and pressed with a folder, is refolded in a reversed direction, in the same creases or edges which had formed the original fold. This discovery was sufficient. It was clear to me that the letter had been turned, as a glove, inside out, re-directed, and resealed. I bade the minister good morning, and took my departure at once, leaving a gold snuff-box upon the table.

"The next morning I called for the snuff-box, when we resumed, quite eagerly, the conversation of the preceding day. While thus engaged, however, a loud report, as if of a pistol, was heard immediately beneath the windows of the hotel, and was succeeded by a series of fearful screams, and the shoutings of a mob. D— rushed to a casement, threw it open, and looked out. In the meantime, I stepped to the card-rack, took the letter, put it in my pocket, and replaced it by a *fac-simile* (so far as regards externals), which I had carefully prepared at my lodgings; imitating the D— cipher, very readily, by means of a seal formed of bread.

"The disturbance in the street had been occasioned by the frantic behaviour of a man with a musket. He had fired it among a crowd of women and children. It proved, however, to have been without ball, and the fellow was suffered to go his way as a lunatic or a drunkard. When he had gone, D— came from the window, whither I had followed him immediately upon securing the object in view. Soon afterwards I bade him farewell. The pretended lunatic was a man in my own pay."

"But what purpose had you," I asked, "in replacing the letter by a *fac-simile*? Would it not have been better, at the first visit, to have seized it openly, and departed?"

"D—," replied Dupin, "is a desperate man, and a man of nerve. His hotel, too, is not without attendants devoted to his interests. Had I made the wild attempt you suggest, I might never have left the ministerial presence alive. The good people of Paris might have heard of me no more. But I had an object apart from these considerations. You know my political prepossessions. In this matter, I act as a partisan of the lady concerned. For eighteen months the minister has had her in his power. She has now him in hers; since, being unaware that the letter is not in his possession, he will proceed with his exactions as if it was. Thus will he inevitably commit himself, at once, to his political destruction. His downfall, too, will not be more precipitate than awkward. It is all very well to talk about the *facilis descensus Averni;* but in all kinds of climbing, as Catalani said of singing, it is far more easy to get up than to come down. In the present instance I have no sympathy—at least no pity— for him who descends. He is that *monstrum horrendum,* an unprincipled man of genius. I confess, however, that I should like very well to know the precise character of his thoughts, when, being defied by her whom the Prefect terms 'a certain personage,' he is reduced to opening the letter which I left for him in the card-rack."

"How? did you put anything particular in it?"

"Why—it did not seem altogether right to leave the interior blank—that would have been insulting. D——, at Vienna once, did me an evil turn, which I told him, quite good-humouredly, that I should remember. So, as I knew he would feel some curiosity in regard to the identity of the person who had outwitted him, I thought it a pity not to give him a clue. He is well acquainted with my MS., and I just copied into the middle of the blank sheet the words—

'—Un dessein si funeste,
S'il n'est digne d'Atrée, est digne de Thyeste.'

They are to be found in Crébillon's *Atrée.*"

THE BRUCE-PARTINGTON PLANS

BY SIR ARTHUR CONAN DOYLE

In the third week of November, in the year 1895, a dense yellow fog settled down upon London. From the Monday to the Thursday I doubt whether it was ever possible from our windows in Baker Street to see the loom of the opposite houses. The first day Holmes had spent in cross-indexing his huge book of references. The second and third had been patiently occupied upon a subject which he had recently made his hobby—the music of the Middle Ages. But when, for the fourth time, after pushing back our chairs from breakfast we saw the greasy, heavy brown swirl still drifting past us and condensing in oily drops upon the window-panes, my comrade's impatient and active nature could endure this drab existence no longer. He paced restlessly about our sitting-room in a fever of suppressed energy, biting his nails, tapping the furniture, and chafing against inaction.

'Nothing of interest in the paper, Watson?' he said.

I was aware that by anything of interest, Holmes meant anything of criminal interest. There was the news of a revolution, of a possible war, and of an impending change of Government; but these did not come within the horizon of my companion. I could see nothing recorded in the shape of crime which was not commonplace and futile. Holmes groaned and resumed his restless meanderings.

'The London criminal is certainly a dull fellow,' said he, in the querulous voice of the sportsman whose game has failed him. 'Look out of this window, Watson. See how the figures loom up, are dimly seen, and then blend once more into the cloud-bank. The thief or the murderer could roam London on such a day as the tiger does the jungle, unseen until he pounces, and then evident only to his victim.'

'There have,' said I, 'been numerous petty thefts.'

Holmes snorted his contempt.

'This great and sombre stage is set for something more worthy than that,' said he. 'It is fortunate for this community that I am not a criminal.'

'It is, indeed!' said I, heartily.

'Suppose that I were Brooks or Woodhouse, or any of the fifty men who have good reason for taking my life, how long could I survive against my own pursuit? A summons, a bogus appointment, and all would be over. It is well they don't have days of fog in the Latin countries—the countries of assassination. By Jove! here comes something at last to break our dead monotony.'

It was the maid with a telegram. Holmes tore it open and burst out laughing.

'Well, well! What next?' said he. 'Brother Mycroft is coming round.'

'Why not?' I asked.

'Why not? It is as if you met a tram-car coming down a country lane. Mycroft has his rails and he runs on them. His Pall Mall lodgings, the Diogenes Club, Whitehall—that is his cycle. Once, and only once, he has been here. What upheaval can possibly have derailed him?'

'Does he not explain?'

Holmes handed me his brother's telegram.

'Must see you over Cadogan West. Coming at once. MYCROFT.'

'Cadogan West? I have heard the name.'

'It recalls nothing to my mind. But that Mycroft should break out in this erratic fashion! A planet might as well leave its orbit. By the way, do you know what Mycroft is?'

I had some vague recollection of an explanation at the time of the Adventure of the Greek Interpreter.

'You told me that he had some small office under the British Government.'

Holmes chuckled.

'I did not know you quite so well in those days. One has to be discreet when one talks of high matters of state. You are right in thinking that he is under the British Government. You would also be right in a sense if you said that occasionally he *is* the British Government.'

'My dear Holmes!'

'I thought I might surprise you. Mycroft draws four hundred and fifty pounds a year, remains a subordinate, has no ambitions of any kind, will receive neither honour nor title, but remains the most indispensable man in the country.'

'But how?'

'Well, his position is unique. He has made it for himself. There has never been anything like it before, nor will be again.

He has the tidiest and most orderly brain, with the greatest capacity for storing facts, of any man living. The same great powers which I have turned to the detection of crime he has used for this particular business. The conclusions of every department are passed to him, and he is the central exchange, the clearing-house, which makes out the balance. All other men are specialists, but his specialism is omniscience. We will suppose that a Minister needs information as to a point which involves the Navy, India, Canada and the bi-metallic question; he could get his separate advices from various departments upon each, but only Mycroft can focus them all, and say off-hand how each factor would affect the other. They began by using him as a short-cut, a convenience; now he has made himself an essential. In that great brain of his everything is pigeon-holed, and can be handed out in an instant. Again and again his word has decided the national policy. He lives in it. He thinks of nothing else save when, as an intellectual exercise, he unbends if I call upon him and ask him to advise me on one of my little problems. But Jupiter is descending to-day. What on earth can it mean? Who is Cadogan West, and what is he to Mycroft?'

'I have it,' I cried, and plunged among the litter of papers upon the sofa. 'Yes, yes, here he is, sure enough! Cadogan West was the young man who was found dead on the Underground on Tuesday morning.'

Holmes sat up at attention, his pipe half-way to his lips.

'This must be serious, Watson. A death which has caused my brother to alter his habits can be no ordinary one. What in the world can he have to do with it? The case was featureless as I remember it. The young man had apparently fallen out of the train and killed himself. He had not been robbed, and there was no particular reason to suspect violence. Is that not so?'

'There has been an inquest,' said I, 'and a good many fresh facts have come out. Looked at more closely, I should certainly say that it was a curious case.'

'Judging by its effect on my brother, I should think it must be a most extraordinary one.' He snuggled down in his armchair. 'Now, Watson, let us have the facts.'

'The man's name was Arthur Cadogan West. He was twenty-seven years of age, unmarried, and a clerk at Woolwich Arsenal.'

'Government employ. Behold the link with brother Mycroft!'

'He left Woolwich suddenly on Monday night. Was last seen by his fiancée, Miss Violet Westbury, whom he left abruptly in the fog about 7.30 that evening. There was no quarrel between them and she can give no motive for his action. The next thing heard of him was when his dead body was discovered by a platelayer named Mason just outside Aldgate Station on the Underground system in London.'

'When?'

'The body was found at six on the Tuesday morning. It was lying wide of the metals upon the left hand of the track as one goes eastward, at a point close to the station, where the line emerges from the tunnel in which it runs. The head was badly crushed—an injury which might well have been caused by a fall from the train. The body could only have come on the line in that way. Had it been carried down from any neighbouring street, it must have passed the station barriers, where a collector is always standing. This point seems absolutely certain.'

'Very good. The case is definite enough. The man, dead or

alive, either fell or was precipitated from the train. So much is clear to me. Continue.'

'The trains which traverse the lines of rail beside which the body was found are those which run from west to east, some being purely Metropolitan, and some from Willesden and out-lying junctions. It can be stated for certain that this young man, when he met his death, was travelling in this direction at some late hour of the night, but at what point he entered the train it is impossible to state.'

'His ticket, of course, would show that.'

'There was no ticket in his pockets.'

'No ticket! Dear me, Watson, this is really very singular. According to my experience it is not possible to reach the platform of a Metropolitan train without exhibiting one's ticket. Presumably, then, the young man had one. Was it taken from him in order to conceal the station from which he came? It is possible. Or did he drop it in the carriage? That also is possible. But the point is of curious interest. I understand that there was no sign of robbery?'

'Apparently not. There is a list here of his possessions. His purse contained two pounds fifteen. He had also a cheque-book on the Woolwich branch of the Capital and Counties Bank. Through this his identity was established. There were also two dress-circle tickets for the Woolwich Theatre, dated for that very evening. Also a small packet of technical papers.'

Holmes gave an exclamation of satisfaction.

'There we have it at last, Watson! British Government—Woolwich Arsenal—Technical papers—Brother Mycroft, the chain is complete. But here he comes, if I am not mistaken, to speak for himself.'

A moment later the tall and portly form of Mycroft Holmes was ushered into the room. Heavily built and massive, there was a suggestion of uncouth physical inertia in the figure, but above this unwieldy frame there was perched a head so masterful in its brow, so alert in its steel-grey, deep-set eyes, so firm in its lips, and so subtle in its play of expression, that after the first glance one forgot the gross body and remembered only the dominant mind.

At his heels came our old friend Lestrade, of Scotland Yard—thin and austere. The gravity of both their faces foretold some weighty quest. The detective shook hands without a word. Mycroft Holmes struggled out of his overcoat and subsided into an arm-chair.

'A most annoying business, Sherlock,' said he. 'I extremely dislike altering my habits, but the powers that be would take no denial. In the present state of Siam it is most awkward that I should be away from the office. But it is a real crisis. I have never seen the Prime Minister so upset. As to the Admiralty—it is buzzing like an overturned beehive. Have you read up the case?'

'We have just done so. What were the technical papers?'

'Ah, there's the point! Fortunately, it has not come out. The Press would be furious if it did. The papers which this wretched youth had in his pocket were the plans of the Bruce-Partington submarine.'

Mycroft Holmes spoke with a solemnity which showed his sense of the importance of the subject. His brother and I sat expectant.

'Surely you have heard of it? I thought everyone had heard of it.'

'Only as a name.'

'Its importance can hardly be exaggerated. It has been the most jealously guarded of all Government secrets. You can take it from me that naval warfare becomes impossible within the radius of a Bruce-Partington's operation. Two years ago a very large sum was smuggled through the Estimates and was expended in acquiring a monopoly of the invention. Every effort has been made to keep the secret. The plans, which are exceedingly intricate, comprising some thirty separate patents, each essential to the working of the whole, are kept in an elaborate safe in a confidential office adjoining the Arsenal, with burglar-proof doors and windows. Under no conceivable circumstances were the plans to be taken from the office. If the Chief Constructor of the Navy desired to consult them, even he was forced to go to the Woolwich office for the purpose. And yet here we find them in the pockets of a dead junior clerk in the heart of London. From an official point of view it's simply awful.'

'But you have recovered them?'

'No, Sherlock, no! That's the pinch. We have not. Ten papers were taken from Woolwich. There were seven in the pockets of Cadogan West. The three most essential are gone—stolen, vanished. You must drop everything, Sherlock. Never mind your usual petty puzzles of the police-court. It's a vital international problem that you have to solve. Why did Cadogan West take the papers, where are the missing ones, how did he die, how came his body where it was found, how can the evil be set right? Find an answer to all these questions, and you will have done good service for your country.'

'Why do you not solve it yourself, Mycroft? You can see as far as I can.'

'Possibly, Sherlock. But it is a question of getting details. Give me your details, and from an arm-chair I will return you an excellent expert opinion. But to run here and run there, to cross-question railway guards, and lie on my face with a lens to my eye—it is not my *métier*. No, you are the one man who can clear the matter up. If you have a fancy to see your name in the next honours list—'

My friend smiled and shook his head.

'I play the game for the game's own sake,' said he. 'But the problem certainly presents some points of interest, and I shall be very pleased to look into it. Some more facts, please.'

'I have jotted down the more essential ones upon this sheet of paper, together with a few addresses which you will find of service. The actual official guardian of the papers is the famous Government expert, Sir James Walter, whose decorations and sub-titles fill two lines of a book of reference. He has grown grey in the service, is a gentleman, a favoured guest in the most exalted houses, and above all a man whose patriotism is beyond suspicion. He is one of two who have a key of the safe. I may add that the papers were undoubtedly in the office during working hours on Monday, and that Sir James left for London about three o'clock taking his key with him. He was at the house of Admiral Sinclair at Barclay Square during the whole of the evening when this incident occurred.'

'Has the fact been verified?'

'Yes; his brother, Colonel Valentine Walter, has testified to his departure from Woolwich, and Admiral Sinclair to his arrival in London; so Sir James is no longer a direct factor in the problem.'

'Who was the other man with a key?'

'The senior clerk and draughtsman, Mr. Sidney Johnson. He is a man of forty, married, with five children. He is a silent, morose man, but he has, on the whole, an excellent record in the public service. He is unpopular with his colleagues, but a hard worker. According to his own account, corroborated only by the word of his wife, he was at home the whole of Monday evening after office hours, and his key has never left the watch-chain upon which it hangs.'

'Tell us about Cadogan West.'

'He has been ten years in the Service, and has done good work. He has the reputation of being hot-headed and impetuous, but a straight, honest man. We have nothing against him. He was next Sidney Johnson in the office. His duties brought him into daily personal contact with the plans. No one else had the handling of them.'

'Who locked the plans up that night?'

'Mr. Sidney Johnson, the senior clerk.'

'Well, it is surely perfectly clear who took them away. They are actually found upon the person of this junior clerk, Cadogan West. That seems final, does it not?'

'It does, Sherlock, and yet it leaves so much unexplained. In the first place, why did he take them?'

'I presume they were of value?'

'He could have got several thousands for them very easily.'

'Can you suggest any possible motive for taking the papers to London except to sell them?'

'No, I cannot.'

'Then we must take that as our working hypothesis. Young West took the papers. Now this could only be done by having a false key—'

'Several false keys. He had to open the building and the room.'

'He had, then, several false keys. He took the papers to London to sell the secret, intending, no doubt, to have the plans themselves back in the safe next morning before they were missed. While in London on this treasonable mission he met his end.'

'How?'

'We will suppose that he was travelling back to Woolwich when he was killed and thrown out of the compartment.'

'Aldgate, where the body was found, is considerably past the station for London Bridge, which would be his route to Woolwich.'

'Many circumstances could be imagined under which he would pass London Bridge. There was someone in the carriage, for example, with whom he was having an absorbing interview. This interview led to a violent scene, in which he lost his life. Possibly he tried to leave the carriage, fell out on the line, and so met his end. The other closed the door. There was a thick fog, and nothing could be seen.'

'No better explanation can be given with our present knowledge; and yet consider, Sherlock, how much you leave untouched. We will suppose, for argument's sake, that young Cadogan West *had* determined to convey these papers to London. He would naturally have made an appointment with the foreign agent and kept his evening clear. Instead of that he took two tickets for the theatre, escorted his fiancée half-way there, and then suddenly disappeared.'

'A blind,' said Lestrade, who had sat listening with some impatience to the conversation.

'A very singular one. That is objection No. 1. Objection No. 2: We will suppose that he reaches London and sees the foreign agent. He must bring back the papers before morning or the loss will be discovered. He took away ten. Only seven were in his pocket. What had become of the other three? He certainly would not leave them of his own free will. Then, again, where is the price of his treason? One would have expected to find a large sum of money in his pocket.'

'It seems to me perfectly clear,' said Lestrade. 'I have no doubt at all as to what occurred. He took the papers to sell them. He saw the agent. They could not agree as to price. He started home again, but the agent went with him. In the train the agent murdered him, took the more essential papers, and threw his body from the carriage. That would account for everything, would it not?'

'Why had he no ticket?'

'The ticket would have shown which station was nearest the agent's house. Therefore he took it from the murdered man's pocket.'

'Good, Lestrade, very good,' said Holmes. 'Your theory holds together. But if this is true, then the case is at an end. On the one hand the traitor is dead. On the other the plans of the Bruce-Partington submarine are presumably already on the Continent. What is there for us to do?'

'To act, Sherlock—to act!' cried Mycroft, springing to his

feet. 'All my instincts are against this explanation. Use your powers! Go to the scene of the crime! See the people concerned! Leave no stone unturned! In all your career you have never had so great a chance of serving your country.'

'Well, well!' said Holmes, shrugging his shoulders. 'Come, Watson! And you, Lestrade, could you favour us with your company for an hour or two? We will begin our investigation by a visit to Aldgate Station. Good-bye, Mycroft. I shall let you have a report before evening, but I warn you in advance that you have little to expect.'

An hour later, Holmes, Lestrade and I stood upon the underground railroad at the point where it emerges from the tunnel immediately before Aldgate Station. A courteous red-faced old gentleman represented the railway company.

'This is where the young man's body lay,' said he, indicating a spot about three feet from the metals. 'It could not have fallen from above, for these, as you see, are all blank walls. Therefore, it could only have come from a train, and that train, so far as we can trace it, must have passed about midnight on Monday.'

'Have the carriages been examined for any sign of violence?'

'There are no such signs, and no ticket has been found.'

'No record of a door being found open?'

'None.'

'We have had some fresh evidence this morning,' said Lestrade. 'A passenger who passed Aldgate in an ordinary Metropolitan train about 11.40 on Monday night declares that he heard a heavy thud, as of a body striking the line, just before the train reached the station. There was dense fog, however, and nothing could be seen. He made no report of it at the time. Why, whatever is the matter with Mr. Holmes?'

My friend was standing with an expression of strained intensity upon his face, staring at the railway metals where they curved out of the tunnel. Aldgate is a junction, and there was a network of points. On these his eager, questioning eyes were fixed, and I saw on his keen, alert face that tightening of the lips, that quiver of the nostrils, and concentration of the heavy tufted brows which I knew so well.

'Points,' he muttered; 'the points.'

'What of it? What do you mean?'

'I suppose there are no great number of points on a system such as this?'

'No; there are very few.'

'And a curve, too. Points, and a curve. By Jove! if it were only so.'

'What is it, Mr. Holmes? Have you a clue?'

'An idea—an indication, no more. But the case certainly grows in interest. Unique, perfectly unique, and yet why not? I do not see any indications of bleeding on the line.'

'There were hardly any.'

'But I understand that there was a considerable wound.'

'The bone was crushed, but there was no great external injury.'

'And yet one would have expected some bleeding. Would it be possible for me to inspect the train which contained the passenger who heard the thud of a fall in the fog?'

'I fear not, Mr. Holmes. The train has been broken up before now, and the carriages redistributed.'

'I can assure you, Mr. Holmes,' said Lestrade, 'that every carriage has been carefully examined. I saw to it myself.'

It was one of my friend's most obvious weaknesses that he was impatient with less alert intelligences than his own.

'Very likely,' said he, turning away. 'As it happens, it was not the carriages which I desired to examine. Watson, we have done all we can here. We need not trouble you any further, Mr. Lestrade. I think our investigations must now carry us to Woolwich.'

At London Bridge, Holmes wrote a telegram to his brother, which he handed to me before dispatching it. It ran thus:

'See some light in the darkness, but it may possibly flicker out. Meanwhile, please send my messenger, to await return at Baker Street, a complete list of all foreign spies or international agents known to be in England, with full address.—SHERLOCK.'

'That should be helpful, Watson,' he remarked, as we took our seats in the Woolwich train. 'We certainly owe brother Mycroft a debt for having introduced us to what promises to be a really very remarkable case.'

His eager face still wore that expression of intense and high-strung energy, which showed me that some novel and suggestive circumstance had opened up a stimulating line of thought. See the foxhound with hanging ears and drooping tail as it lolls about the kennels, and compare it with the same hound as, with gleaming eyes and straining muscles, it runs upon a breast-high scent—such was the change in Holmes since the morning. He was a different man to the limp and lounging figure in the mouse-coloured dressing-gown who had prowled so restlessly only a few hours before round the fog-girt room.

'There is material here. There is scope,' said he. 'I am dull indeed not to have understood its possibilities.'

'Even now they are dark to me.'

'The end is dark to me also, but I have hold of one idea which may lead us far. The man met his death elsewhere, and his body was on the *roof* of a carriage.'

'On the roof!'

'Remarkable, is it not? But consider the facts. Is it a coincidence that it is found at the very point where the train pitches and sways as it comes round on the points? Is not that the place where an object upon the roof might be expected to fall off? The points would affect no object inside the train. Either the body fell from the roof, or a very curious coincidence has occurred. But now consider the question of the blood. Of course, there was no bleeding on the line if the body had bled elsewhere. Each fact is suggestive in itself. Together they have a cumulative force.'

'And the ticket, too!' I cried.

'Exactly. We could not explain the absence of a ticket. This would explain it. Everything fits together.'

'But suppose it were so, we are still as far as ever from unravelling the mystery of his death. Indeed, it becomes not simpler, but stranger.'

'Perhaps,' said Holmes, thoughtfully; 'perhaps.' He relapsed into a silent reverie, which lasted until the slow train drew up at last in Woolwich Station. There he called a cab and drew Mycroft's paper from his pocket.

'We have quite a little round of afternoon calls to make,' said he. 'I think that Sir James Walter claims our first attention.'

The house of the famous official was a fine villa with green lawns stretching down to the Thames. As we reached it the fog was lifting, and a thin, watery sunshine was breaking through. A butler answered our ring.

'Sir James, sir!' said he, with solemn face. 'Sir James died this morning.'

'Good heavens!' cried Holmes, in amazement. 'How did he die?'

'Perhaps you would care to step in, sir, and see his brother, Colonel Valentine?'

'Yes, we had best do so.'

We were ushered into a dim-lit drawing-room, where an instant later we were joined by a very tall, handsome, light-bearded man of fifty, the younger brother of the dead scientist. His wild eyes, stained cheeks, and unkempt hair all spoke of the sudden blow which had fallen upon the household. He was hardly articulate as he spoke of it.

'It was this horrible scandal,' said he. 'My brother, Sir James, was a man of very sensitive honour, and he could not survive such an affair. It broke his heart. He was always so proud of the efficiency of his department, and this was a crushing blow.'

'We had hoped that he might have given us some indications which would have helped us to clear the matter up.'

'I assure you that it was all a mystery to him as it is to you and to all of us. He had already put all his knowledge at the disposal of the police. Naturally, he had no doubt that Cadogan West was guilty. But all the rest was inconceivable.'

'You cannot throw any new light upon the affair?'

'I know nothing myself save what I have read or heard. I have no desire to be discourteous, but you can understand, Mr. Holmes, that we are much disturbed at present, and I must ask you to hasten this interview to an end.'

'This is indeed an unexpected development,' said my friend when we had regained the cab. 'I wonder if the death was natural, or whether the poor old fellow killed himself! If the latter, may it be taken as some sign of self-reproach for duty neglected? We must leave that question to the future. Now we shall turn to the Cadogan Wests.'

A small but well-kept house in the outskirts of the town sheltered the bereaved mother. The old lady was too dazed with grief to be of any use to us, but at her side was a white-faced young lady, who introduced herself as Miss Violet Westbury, the fiancée of the dead man, and the last to see him upon that fatal night.

'I cannot explain it, Mr. Holmes,' she said. 'I have not shut an eye since the tragedy, thinking, thinking, thinking, night and day, what the true meaning of it can be. Arthur was the most single-minded, chivalrous, patriotic man upon earth. He would have cut his right hand off before he would sell a State secret confided to his keeping. It is absurd, impossible, preposterous to anyone who knew him.'

'But the facts, Miss Westbury?'

'Yes, yes; I admit I cannot explain them.'

'Was he in any want of money?'

'No; his needs were very simple and his salary ample. He had saved a few hundreds, and we were to marry at the New Year.'

'No signs of any mental excitement? Come, Miss Westbury, be absolutely frank with us.'

The quick eye of my companion had noted some change in her manner. She coloured and hesitated.

'Yes,' she said at last. 'I had a feeling that there was something on his mind.'

'For long?'

'Only for the last week or so. He was thoughtful and worried. Once I pressed him about it. He admitted that there was something, and that it was concerned with his official life. "It is too serious for me to speak about, even to you," said he. I could get nothing more.'

Holmes looked grave.

'Go on, Miss Westbury. Even if it seems to tell against him, go on. We cannot say what it may lead to.'

'Indeed I have nothing more to tell. Once or twice it seemed to me that he was on the point of telling me something. He spoke one evening of the importance of the secret, and I have some recollection that he said that no doubt foreign spies would pay a great deal to have it.'

My friend's face grew graver still.

'Anything else?'

'He said that we were slack about such matters—that it would be easy for a traitor to get the plans.'

'Was it only recently that he made such remarks?'

'Yes, quite recently.'

'Now tell us of that last evening.'

'We were to go to the theatre. The fog was so thick that a cab was useless. We walked, and our way took us close to the office. Suddenly he darted away into the fog.'

'Without a word?'

'He gave an exclamation; that was all. I waited but he never returned. Then I walked home. Next morning, after the office opened, they came to inquire. About twelve o'clock we heard the terrible news. Oh, Mr. Holmes, if you could only, only save his honour! It was so much to him.'

Holmes shook his head sadly.

'Come, Watson,' said he, 'our ways lie elsewhere. Our next station must be the office from which the papers were taken.'

'It was black enough before against this young man, but our inquiries make it blacker,' he remarked, as the cab lumbered off. 'His coming marriage gives a motive for the crime. He naturally wanted money. The idea was in his head, since he spoke about it. He nearly made the girl an accomplice in the treason by telling her his plans. It is all very bad.'

'But surely, Holmes, character goes for something? Then, again, why should he leave the girl in the street and dart away to commit a felony?'

'Exactly! There are certainly objections. But it is a formidable case which they have to meet.'

Mr. Sidney Johnson, the senior clerk, met us at the office, and received us with that respect which my companion's card always commanded. He was a thin, gruff, bespectacled man of middle age, his cheeks haggard, and his hands twitching from the nervous strain to which he had been subjected.

'It is bad, Mr. Holmes, very bad! Have you heard of the death of the Chief?'

'We have just come from his house.'

'The place is disorganised. The Chief dead, Cadogan West dead, our papers stolen. And yet, when we closed our door on Monday evening we were as efficient an office as any in the

Government service. Good God, it's dreadful to think of! That West, of all men, should have done such a thing!'

'You are sure of his guilt, then?'

'I can see no other way out of it. And yet I would have trusted him as I trust myself.'

'At what hour was the office closed on Monday?'

'At five.'

'Did you close it?'

'I am always the last man out.'

'Where were the plans?'

'In that safe. I put them there myself.'

'Is there no watchman to the building?'

'There is; but he has other departments to look after as well. He is an old soldier and a most trustworthy man. He saw nothing that evening. Of course, the fog was very thick.'

'Suppose that Cadogan West wished to make his way into the building after hours; he would need three keys, would he not, before he could reach the papers?'

'Yes, he would. The key of the outer door, the key of the office, and the key of the safe.'

'Only Sir James Walter and you had those keys?'

'I had no keys of the doors—only of the safe.'

'Was Sir James a man who was orderly in his habits?'

'Yes, I think he was. I know that so far as those three keys are concerned he kept them on the same ring. I have often seen them there.'

'And that ring went with him to London?'

'He said so.'

'And your key never left your possession?'

'Never.'

'Then West, if he is the culprit, must have had a duplicate. And yet none was found upon his body. One other point: if a clerk in this office desired to sell the plans, would it not be simpler to copy the plans for himself than to take the originals, as was actually done?'

'It would take considerable technical knowledge to copy the plans in an effective way.'

'But I suppose either Sir James, or you, or West had that technical knowledge?'

'No doubt we had, but I beg you won't try to drag me into the matter, Mr. Holmes. What is the use of our speculating in this way when the original plans were actually found on West?'

'Well, it is certainly singular that he should run the risk of taking originals, if he could safely have taken copies, which would have equally served his turn.'

'Singular, no doubt—and yet he did so.'

'Every inquiry in this case reveals something inexplicable. Now there are three papers still missing. They are, as I understand, the vital ones.'

'Yes, that is so.'

'Do you mean to say that anyone holding these three papers, and without the seven others, could construct a Bruce-Partington submarine?'

'I reported to that effect to the Admiralty. But to-day I have been over the drawings again, and I am not so sure of it. The double valves with the automatic self-adjusting slots are drawn in one of the papers which have been returned. Until the foreigners had invented that for themselves they could not make the boat. Of course, they might soon get over the difficulty.'

'But the three missing drawings are the most important?'

'Undoubtedly.'

'I think, with your permission, I will now take a stroll round the premises. I do not recall any other question which I desired to ask.'

He examined the lock of the safe, the door of the room, and finally the iron shutters of the window. It was only when we were on the lawn outside that his interest was strongly excited. There was a laurel bush outside the window, and several of the branches bore signs of having been twisted or snapped. He examined them carefully with his lens, and then some dim and vague marks upon the earth beneath. Finally he asked the chief clerk to close the iron shutters, and he pointed out to me that they hardly met in the centre, and that it would be possible for anyone outside to see what was going on within the room.

'The indications are ruined by the three days' delay. They may mean something or nothing. Well, Watson, I do not think that Woolwich can help us further. It is a small crop which we have gathered. Let us see if we can do better in London.'

Yet we added one more sheaf to our harvest before we left Woolwich Station. The clerk in the ticket office was able to say with confidence that he saw Cadogan West—whom he knew well by sight—upon the Monday night, and that he went to London by the 8.15 to London Bridge. He was alone, and took a single third-class ticket. The clerk was struck at the time by his excited and nervous manner. So shaky was he that he could hardly pick up his change, and the clerk had helped him with it. A reference to the time-table showed that the 8.15 was the first train which it was possible for West to take after he had left the lady about 7.30.

'Let us reconstruct, Watson,' said Holmes, after half an hour of silence. 'I am not aware that in all our joint researches we have ever had a case which was more difficult to get at. Every fresh advance which we make only reveals a fresh ridge beyond. And yet we have surely made some appreciable progress.

'The effect of our inquiries at Woolwich has in the main been against young Cadogan West; but the indications at the window would lend themselves to a more favourable hypothesis. Let us suppose, for example, that he had been approached by some foreign agent. It might have been done under such pledges as would have prevented him from speaking of it, and yet would have affected his thoughts in the direction indicated by his remarks to his fiancée. Very good. We will now suppose that as he went to the theatre with the young lady he suddenly, in the fog, caught a glimpse of this same agent going in the direction of the office. He was an impetuous man, quick in his decisions. Everything gave way to his duty. He followed the man, reached the window, saw the abstraction of the documents, and pursued the thief. In this way we get over the objection that no one would take originals when he could make copies. This outsider had to take originals. So far it holds together.'

'What is the next step?'

'Then we come into difficulties. One would imagine that under such circumstances the first act of young Cadogan West would be to seize the villain and raise the alarm. Why did he not do so? Could it have been an official superior who took the papers? That would explain West's conduct. Or could the Chief have given West the slip in the fog, and West started at once to London to head him off from his own rooms, presuming that he knew where the rooms were? The call must have been very pressing, since he left his girl standing in the fog, and made no effort to communicate with her. Our scent runs cold here, and there is a vast gap between either hypothesis and the laying of West's body, with seven papers in his pocket, on the roof of a Metropolitan train. My instinct now is to work from the other end. If Mycroft has given us the list of addresses we may be able to pick our man, and follow two tracks instead of one.'

Surely enough, a note awaited us at Baker Street. A Government messenger had brought it post-haste. Holmes glanced at it and threw it over to me.

'There are numerous small fry, but few who would handle so big an affair. The only men worth considering are Adolph Meyer, of 13 Great George Street, Westminster; Louis La Rothière, of Campden Mansions, Notting Hill; and Hugo Oberstein, 13 Caulfield Gardens, Kensington. The latter was known to be in town on Monday, and is now reported as having left. Glad to hear you have seen some light. The Cabinet awaits your final report with the utmost anxiety. Urgent representations have arrived from the very highest quarter. The whole force of the State is at your back if you should need it—MYCROFT.'

'I'm afraid,' said Holmes, smiling, 'that all the Queen's horses and all the Queen's men cannot avail in this matter.' He had spread out his big map of London, and leaned eagerly over it. 'Well, well,' said he presently, with an exclamation of satisfaction, 'things are turning a little in our direction at last. Why, Watson, I do honestly believe that we are going to pull it off after all.' He slapped me on the shoulder with a sudden burst of hilarity. 'I am going out now. It is only a reconnaissance. I will do nothing serious without my trusted comrade and biographer at my elbow. Do you stay here, and the odds are that you will see me again in an hour or two. If time hangs heavy get foolscap and a pen, and begin your narrative of how we saved the State.'

I felt some reflection of his elation in my own mind, for I knew well that he would not depart so far from his usual austerity of demeanour unless there was good cause for exultation. All the long November evening I waited, filled with impatience for his return. At last, shortly after nine o'clock there arrived a messenger with a note:

'Am dining at Goldini's Restaurant, Gloucester Road, Kensington. Please come at once and join me there. Bring with you a jemmy, a dark lantern, a chisel, and a revolver.—S.H.'

It was a nice equipment for a respectable citizen to carry through the dim, fog-draped streets. I stowed them all discreetly away in my overcoat, and drove straight to the address given. There sat my friend at a little round table near the door of the garish Italian restaurant.

'Have you had something to eat? Then join me in a coffee and curaçao. Try one of the proprietor's cigars. They are less poisonous than one would expect. Have you the tools?'

'They are here, in my overcoat.'

'Excellent. Let me give you a short sketch of what I have done, with some indication of what we are about to do. Now it must be evident to you, Watson, that this young man's body was *placed* on the roof of the train. That was clear from the instant that I determined the fact that it was from the roof, and not from a carriage, that he had fallen.'

'Could it not have been dropped from a bridge?'

'I should say it was impossible. If you examine the roofs you will find that they are slightly rounded, and there is no railing round them. Therefore, we can say for certain that young Cadogan West was placed on it.'

'How could he be placed there?'

'That was the question which we had to answer. There is only one possible way. You are aware that the Underground runs clear of tunnels at some points in the West End. I had a vague memory that as I have travelled by it I have occasionally seen windows just above my head. Now, suppose that a train halted under such a window, would there be any difficulty in laying a body upon the roof?'

'It seems most improbable.'

'We must fall back upon the old axiom that when all other contingencies fail, whatever remains, however improbable, must be the truth. Here all other contingencies *have* failed. When I found that the leading international agent, who had just left London, lived in a row of houses which abutted upon the Underground, I was so pleased that you were a little astonished at my sudden frivolity.'

'Oh, that was it, was it?'

'Yes, that was it. Mr. Hugo Oberstein, of 13 Caulfield Gardens, had become my objective. I began my operations at Gloucester Road Station, where a very helpful official walked with me along the track, and allowed me to satisfy myself, not only that the back-stair windows of Caulfield Gardens open on the line, but the even more essential fact that, owing to the intersection of one of the larger railways, the Underground trains are frequently held motionless for some minutes at that very spot.'

'Splendid, Holmes! You have got it!'

'So far—so far, Watson. We advance, but the goal is afar. Well, having seen the back of Caulfield Gardens, I visited the front and satisfied myself that the bird was indeed flown. It is a considerable house, unfurnished, so far as I could judge, in the upper rooms. Oberstein lived there with a single valet, who was probably a confederate entirely in his confidence. We must bear in mind that Oberstein has gone to the Continent to dispose of his booty, but not with any idea of flight; for he had no reason to fear a warrant, and the idea of an amateur domiciliary visit would certainly never occur to him. Yet that is precisely what we are about to make.'

'Could we not get a warrant and legalise it?'

'Hardly on the evidence.'

'What can we hope to do?'

'We cannot tell what correspondence may be there.'

'I don't like it, Holmes.'

'My dear fellow, you shall keep watch in the street. I'll do the criminal part. It's not a time to stick at trifles. Think of Mycroft's note, of the Admiralty, the Cabinet, the exalted person who waits for news. We are bound to go.'

My answer was to rise from the table.

'You are right, Holmes. We are bound to go.'

He sprang up and shook me by the hand.

'I knew you would not shrink at the last,' said he, and for a moment I saw something in his eyes which was nearer to tenderness than I had ever seen. The next instant he was his masterful, practical self once more.

'It is nearly half a mile, but there is no hurry. Let us walk,' said he. 'Don't drop the instruments, I beg. Your arrest as a suspicious character would be a most unfortunate complication.'

Caulfield Gardens was one of those lines of flat-faced, pillared, and porticoed houses which are so prominent a product of the middle Victorian epoch in the West End of London. Next door there appeared to be a children's party, for the merry buzz of young voices and the clatter of a piano resounded through the night. The fog still hung about and screened us with its friendly shade. Holmes had lit his lantern and flashed it upon the massive door.

'This is a serious proposition,' said he. 'It is certainly bolted as well as locked. We would do better in the area. There is an excellent archway down yonder in case a too zealous policeman should intrude. Give me a hand, Watson, and I'll do the same for you.'

A minute later we were both in the area. Hardly had we reached the dark shadows before the step of the policeman was heard in the fog above. As its soft rhythm died away, Holmes set to work upon the lower door. I saw him stoop and strain until with a sharp crash it flew open. We sprang through into the dark passage, closing the area door behind us. Holmes led the way up the curving, uncarpeted stair. His little fan of yellow light shone upon a low window.

'Here we are, Watson—this must be the one.' He threw it open, and as he did so there was a low, harsh murmur, growing steadily into a loud roar as a train dashed past us in the darkness. Holmes swept his light along the window-sill. It was thickly coated with soot from the passing engines, but the black surface was blurred and rubbed in places.

'You can see where they rested the body. Halloa, Watson! what is this? There can be no doubt that it is a blood mark.' He was pointing to faint discolourations along the woodwork of the window. 'Here it is on the stone of the stair also. The demonstration is complete. Let us stay here until a train stops.'

We had not long to wait. The very next train roared from the tunnel as before, but slowed in the open, and then, with a creaking of brakes, pulled up immediately beneath us. It was not four feet from the window-ledge to the roof of the carriages. Holmes softly closed the window.

'So far we are justified,' said he. 'What do you think of it, Watson?'

'A masterpiece. You have never risen to a greater height.'

'I cannot agree with you there. From the moment that I conceived the idea of the body being upon the roof, which surely was not a very abstruse one, all the rest was inevitable. If it were not for the grave interests involved the affair up to this point would be insignificant. Our difficulties are still before us. But perhaps we may find something here which may help us.'

We had ascended the kitchen stair and entered the suite of rooms upon the first floor. One was a dining-room, severely furnished and containing nothing of interest. A second was a bedroom, which also drew blank. The remaining room appeared more promising, and my companion settled down to a systematic examination. It was littered with books and papers, and was evidently used as a study. Swiftly and methodically Holmes turned over the contents of drawer after drawer and cupboard after cupboard, but no gleam of success came to brighten his austere face. At the end of an hour he was no further than when he started.

'The cunning dog has covered his tracks,' said he. 'He has left nothing to incriminate him. His dangerous correspondence has been destroyed or removed. This is our last chance.'

It was a small tin cash-box which stood upon the writing-desk. Holmes prised it open with his chisel. Several rolls of paper were within, covered with figures and calculations, without any note to show to what they referred. The recurring words, 'Water pressure,' and 'Pressure to the square inch' suggested some possible relation to a submarine. Holmes tossed them all impatiently aside. There only remained an envelope with some small newspaper slips inside it. He shook them out on the table, and at once I saw by his eager face that his hopes had been raised.

'What's this, Watson? Eh? What's this? Record of a series of messages in the advertisements of a paper. *Daily Telegraph* agony column by the print and paper. Right-hand top corner of a page. No dates—but messages arrange themselves. This must be the first:

' "Hoped to hear sooner. Terms agreed to. Write fully to address given on card.—Pierrot."

'Next comes: "Matter presses. Must withdraw offer unless contract completed. Make appointment by letter. Will confirm by advertisement.—Pierrot."

'Finally: "Monday night after nine. Two taps. Only ourselves. Do not be so suspicious. Payment in hard cash when goods delivered.—Pierrot."

'A fairly complete record, Watson! If we could only get at the man at the other end!' He sat lost in thought, tapping his fingers on the table. Finally he sprang to his feet.

'Well, perhaps it won't be so difficult after all. There is nothing more to be done here, Watson. I think we might drive round to the offices of the *Daily Telegraph,* and so bring a good day's work to a conclusion.'

Mycroft Holmes and Lestrade had come round by appointment after breakfast next day and Sherlock Holmes had recounted to them our proceedings of the day before. The professional shook his head over our confessed burglary.

'We can't do these things in the force, Mr. Holmes,' said he. 'No wonder you get results that are beyond us. But some of these days you'll go too far, and you'll find yourself and your friend in trouble.'

'For England, home and beauty—eh, Watson? Martyrs on the altar of our country. But what do you think of it, Mycroft?'

'Excellent, Sherlock! Admirable! But what use will you make of it?'

Holmes picked up the *Daily Telegraph* which lay upon the table.

'Have you seen Pierrot's advertisement to-day?'

'What! Another one?'

'Yes, here it is: "To-night. Same hour. Same place. Two taps. Most vitally important. Your own safety at stake.—Pierrot."'

'By George!' cried Lestrade. 'If he answers that we've got him!'

'That was my idea when I put it in. I think if you could both make it convenient to come with us about eight o'clock to Caulfield Gardens we might possibly get a little nearer to a solution.'

One of the most remarkable characteristics of Sherlock Holmes was his power of throwing his brain out of action and switching all his thoughts on to lighter things whenever he had convinced himself that he could no longer work to advantage. I remember that during the whole of that memorable day he lost himself in a monograph which he had undertaken upon the Polyphonic Motets of Lassus. For my own part I had none of this power of detachment, and the day, in consequence, appeared to be interminable. The great national importance of the issue, the suspense in high quarters, the direct nature of the experiment which we were trying—all combined to work upon my nerve. It was a relief to me when at last, after a light dinner, we set out upon our expedition. Lestrade and Mycroft met us by appointment at the outside of Gloucester Road Station. The area door of Oberstein's house had been left open the night before, and it was necessary for me, as Mycroft Holmes absolutely and indignantly declined to climb the railings, to pass in and open the hall door. By nine o'clock we were all seated in the study, waiting patiently for our man.

An hour passed and yet another. When eleven struck, the measured beat of the great church clock seemed to sound the dirge of our hopes. Lestrade and Mycroft were fidgeting in their seats and looking twice a minute at their watches. Holmes sat silent and composed, his eyelids half shut, but every sense on the alert. He raised his head with a sudden jerk.

'He is coming,' said he.

There had been a furtive step past the door. Now it returned. We heard a shuffling sound outside, and then two sharp taps with the knocker. Holmes rose, motioning to us to remain seated. The gas in the hall was a mere point of light. He opened the outer door, and then as a dark figure slipped past him he closed and fastened it. 'This way!' we heard him say, and a moment later our man stood before us. Holmes had followed him closely, and as the man turned with a cry of surprise and alarm he caught him by the collar and threw him back into the room. Before our prisoner had recovered his balance the door was shut and Holmes standing with his back against it. The man glared round him, staggered, and fell senseless upon the floor. With the shock, his broad-brimmed hat flew from his head, his cravat slipped down from his lips, and there was a long light beard and the soft, handsome delicate features of Colonel Valentine Walter.

Holmes gave a whistle of surprise.

'You can write me down an ass this time, Watson,' said he. 'This was not the bird that I was looking for.'

'Who is he?' asked Mycroft eagerly.

'The younger brother of the late Sir James Walter, the head of the Submarine Department. Yes, yes; I see the fall of the cards. He is coming to. I think that you had best leave his examination to me.'

We had carried the prostrate body to the sofa. Now our prisoner sat up, looked round him with a horror-stricken face, and passed his hand over his forehead, like one who cannot believe his own senses.

'What is this?' he asked. 'I came here to visit Mr. Oberstein.'

'Everything is known, Colonel Walter,' said Holmes. 'How an English gentleman could behave in such a manner is beyond my comprehension. But your whole correspondence and relations with Oberstein are within our knowledge. So also are the circumstances connected with the death of young Cadogan West. Let me advise you to gain at least the small credit for repentance and confession, since there are still some details which we can only learn from your lips.'

The man groaned and sank his face in his hands. We waited, but he was silent.

'I can assure you,' said Holmes, 'that every essential is already known. We know that you were pressed for money; that you took an impress of the keys which your brother held; and that you entered into a correspondence with Oberstein, who answered your letters through the advertisement columns of the *Daily Telegraph*. We are aware that you went down to the office in the fog on Monday night, but that you were seen and followed by young Cadogan West, who had probably some previous reason to suspect you. He saw your theft, but could not give the alarm, as it was just possible that you were taking the papers to your brother in London. Leaving all his private concerns, like the good citizen that he was, he followed you closely in the fog, and kept at your heels until you reached this very house. There he intervened, and then it was, Colonel Walter, that to treason you added the more terrible crime of murder.'

'I did not! I did not! Before God I swear that I did not!' cried our wretched prisoner.

'Tell us, then, how Cadogan West met his end before you

laid him upon the roof of a railway carriage.'

'I will. I swear to you that I will. I did the rest. I confess it. It was just as you say. A Stock Exchange debt had to be paid. I needed the money badly. Oberstein offered me five thousand. It was to save myself from ruin. But as to murder, I am as innocent as you.'

'What happened then?'

'He had his suspicions before, and he followed me as you describe. I never knew it until I was at the very door. It was thick fog, and one could not see three yards. I had given two taps and Oberstein had come to the door. The young man rushed up and demanded to know what we were about to do with the papers. Oberstein had a short life-preserver. He always carried it with him. As West forced his way after us into the house Oberstein struck him on the head. The blow was a fatal one. He was dead within five minutes. There he lay in the hall, and we were at our wits' end what to do. Then Oberstein had this idea about the trains which halted under his back window. But first he examined the papers which I had brought. He said that three of them were essential, and that he must keep them. "You cannot keep them," said I. "There will be a dreadful row at Woolwich if they are not returned." "I must keep them," said he, "for they are so technical that it is impossible in the time to make copies." "Then they must all go back together to-night," said I. He thought for a little, and then he cried out that he had it. "Three I will keep," said he. "The others we will stuff into the pocket of this young man. When he is found the whole business will assuredly be put to his account." I could see no other way out of it, so we did as he suggested. We waited half an hour at the window before a train stopped. It was so thick that nothing could be seen, and we had no difficulty in lowering West's body on to the train. That was the end of the matter so far as I was concerned.'

'And your brother?'

'He said nothing, but he had caught me once with his keys, and I think that he suspected. I read in his eyes that he suspected. As you know, he never held up his head again.'

There was silence in the room. It was broken by Mycroft Holmes.

'Can you not make reparation? It would ease your conscience, and possibly your punishment.'

'What reparation can I make?'

'Where is Oberstein with the papers?'

'I do not know.'

'Did he give you no address?'

'He said that letters to the Hôtel du Louvre, Paris, would eventually reach him.'

'Then reparation is still within your power,' said Sherlock Holmes.

'I will do anything I can. I owe this fellow no particular goodwill. He has been my ruin and my downfall.'

'Here are paper and pen. Sit at this desk and write to my dictation. Direct the envelope to the address given. That is right. Now the letter: "Dear Sir,—With regard to our transaction, you will no doubt have observed by now that one essential detail is missing. I have a tracing which will make it complete. This has involved me in extra trouble, however, and I must ask you for a further advance of five hundred pounds. I will not trust it to the post, nor will I take anything but gold or notes. I would come to you abroad, but it would excite remark if I left the country at present. Therefore I shall expect to meet you in the smoking-room of the Charing Cross Hotel at noon on Saturday. Remember that only English notes, or gold, will be taken." That will do very well. I shall be very much surprised if it does not fetch our man.'

And it did! It is a matter of history—that secret history of a nation which is often so much more intimate and interesting than its public chronicles—that Oberstein, eager to complete the coup of his lifetime, came to the lure and was safely engulfed for fifteen years in a British prison. In his trunk were found the invaluable Bruce-Partington plans, which he had put up for auction in all the naval centres of Europe.

Colonel Walter died in prison towards the end of the second year of his sentence. As to Holmes, he returned refreshed to his monograph upon the Polyphonic Motets of Lassus, which has since been printed for private circulation, and is said by experts to be the last word upon the subject. Some weeks afterwards I learned incidentally that my friend spent a day at Windsor, whence he returned with a remarkably fine emerald tie-pin. When I asked him if he had bought it, he answered that it was a present from a certain gracious lady in whose interests he had once been fortunate enough to carry out a small commission. He said no more; but I fancy that I could guess at that lady's august name, and I have little doubt that the emerald pin will for ever recall to my friend's memory the adventure of the Bruce-Partington plans.

THE BRASS BUTTERFLY

BY WILLIAM LE QUEUX

The affair of the Brass Butterfly was kept a profound secret for reasons which will be obvious.

Late on the night of 6th December 1906, I alighted at the big echoing station of Bologna, after a long and tedious journey from Charing Cross.

I was, as usual, on a secret mission, and there were strong reasons why I should not go to the Hôtel Brun or any of the other first-class houses frequented by British tourists, therefore I drove to an obscure little inn situated up a back street, called the Hôtel Tazza d'Oro. You may have seen it, a dark, frowsy, little place, dingy and so obviously unclean that, as an Englishman, you would have shuddered at the mere thought of passing a night there.

But I was not desirous of being recognised by certain persons to whom I was known in that city, therefore I registered my name as Pietro Pirelli, commercial traveller, of Naples.

I was there in order to solve a problem which had considerably puzzled us at Whitehall.

I glanced around the shabby, unclean room to which I was shown, washed my hands, and then sauntered forth along those long dark colonnaded streets that are the same today as they were back in the Middle Ages, until I had crossed the broad moonlit Piazza before the Duomo, and plunged into a maze of narrow thoroughfares which brought me eventually into a wider medieval street in front of a great, dark, almost prison-like palace of the *cinquecento* with a coat-of-arms graven in stone over the arched gateway closed by a ponderous iron-studded door.

It was the Palazzo Bardi, wherein lived the Donna Stella, the twenty-year-old daughter of the great Marquis Bardi, the millionaire landowner and Senator of the Kingdom of Italy.

The windows of the huge square stone building, almost a fortress, were closely shuttered and barred, a grim, silent place which none would believe contained such priceless works of art, or one of the most famous collections of armour in the world.

I crossed the road to the big ancient door which had withstood many a siege in those turbulent days when the Bardi so constantly fought the Ginestrelli from Pistoja, across the Apennines. Then, switching on the light of my little electric lamp, I stood on tiptoe and carefully examined the antique bronze knocker in the form of the grinning face of a satyr.

Upon one of the polished cheeks of the grotesque mask I found what I sought—a small cross, scratched by a pin.

Then, well satisfied, I turned upon my heel and retraced my steps to my obscure hotel. The Donna Stella had received my message in safety, and would meet me in secret next day.

When at noon I stood at a remote spot in the little park beyond the city, awaiting her, she came, a slim, neat-waisted figure in black, accompanied by 'Spot', her English fox-terrier. A smile of welcome lit up her handsome face as she placed her gloved hand in mine in greeting.

'You are, no doubt, surprised, signorina, at my sudden appearance in Bologna,' I said. 'But it is, in a great measure, in your interests.'

'In mine! I don't understand!' she replied in excellent English, for she had been educated at Brighton.

'In the interests of your friend Captain Devrill,' I said quietly.

Her face changed instantly.

'Have you heard anything of him? Have you just come from Vienna?'

'Unfortunately I am entirely without information,' I said. 'My friend has mysteriously disappeared.'

Jack Devrill, ex-captain of Royal Engineers, and one of the most alert and active of my colleagues, was her particular friend. They had met in England when she was still a schoolgirl, and their friendship had ripened into affection. Yet a great gulf lay between them, for it was hardly likely that she, only daughter and heiress of one of the wealthiest Roman nobles and niece of Prince von Furstenberg, the great Austrian statesman who held the office of Imperial and Royal Minister for Foreign Affairs, and who ruled at the Ballhausplatz, the Foreign Office at Vienna, would be allowed to marry the careless cosmopolitan Secret Service agent.

'I have been waiting in daily anxiety for news of him,' she sighed. 'I cannot understand it. Ah! Mr Morrice, you cannot know in what terror and dread I have existed, ever since I left Vienna twelve days ago. I—I fear that something terrible has happened to him!'

This was exactly the opinion of our Department. Jack Devrill had disappeared into space; he had fallen the victim of some enemy—betrayed, without a doubt.

The facts were briefly these. Sixteen days ago Jack and I had arrived in Vienna on a most important and secret mission. Suspicion had been aroused that something unusual was afoot at the Ballhausplatz, and we had been dispatched from Whitehall to endeavour to ascertain what was in progress.

In the gay Austrian capital we were both well-known, so we at once left cards and received many invitations. I had served as an attaché there four years before, hence I knew a great many of the officials. We lived at the Hôtel Bristol, as was our habit, and the Donna Stella being on a visit to her uncle, we were both invited several times to the great official residence of the Foreign Minister in the Franzens Ring. On one of these brilliant occasions—an official ball at which the white-bearded Emperor and his suite were present—I accompanied Devrill. Donna Stella, with whom I waltzed once, looked inexpressibly dainty in turquoise chiffon, but soon afterwards I missed the pair, and concluded that they were sitting out.

That night, however, Jack mysteriously disappeared. Enquiries I made of the night-porter at the hotel next day showed that my friend had returned at about two-thirty, changed his clothes, and an hour later had gone forth—whither no one knew. I had returned an hour afterwards, but had been unaware that he was missing till near noon.

I went to his room, and there found all his belongings in perfect order, but on the table there stood a quaint antique object which he had evidently bought only a few hours before going to the ball—an old Turkish ornament in which to burn perfume—a big butterfly of polished brass.

It measured about a foot across from tip to tip of its wings, fashioned beautifully, the body perforated to allow the fragrance of the smoking pastilles to escape into the room. I examined it minutely. There was a cavity along the body, but nothing was inside. I saw at once that he had evidently bought it to add to the collection of antiques he possessed at his cosy rooms in Half Moon Street. I wondered, however, why he had not shown it to me. Whether it was on account of its unusual grotesqueness, or the delicacy of its design, I know not, yet I somehow became unusually attracted by my friend's curious purchase, and took it to an antique dealer in the Burggasse, who pronounced it to be a rare specimen of sixteenth-century work, probably from the harem of some rich pasha in the south of Turkey.

I grew alarmed at the non-return of my friend, and reported his disappearance by cipher to that cryptic telegraphic address in London with which we are so constantly communicating. My orders were to spare no effort to clear up the mystery. As far as could be ascertained, the political horizon was perfectly unclouded. Yet the fact of Jack's disappearance had considerably strengthened our suspicions.

'What effort has been made to find him?' asked the girl anxiously.

'Every effort, signorina. The police of the whole Austrian Empire are in active search for traces of him.'

'What can I do?' she asked hoarsely, pale-faced and anxious. 'This silence of his means foul play—of that I now feel convinced.'

That was exactly my opinion, though I did not admit it. Jack Devrill would certainly have reported himself ere that, by sending his name to the deaths column of *The Times* 'In memoriam'.

'I'm here, signorina,' I said, 'to ask you a question. Pardon my inquisitiveness, but it is in Devrill's interests. On the night of the ball at His Excellency's both you and he were absent from the room after eleven o'clock. Were you sitting with him the whole time?'

Her face blanched, then flushed crimson. At first she became confused, then indignant at my question.

'I really cannot see what that had to do with it,' she answered resentfully, surprising me by her antagonistic attitude. Over her handsome countenance was a cloud of undisguised displeasure that I should ask such a question.

'I am trying to solve the cause of Jack's disappearance,' I said quietly. 'Cannot you be frank with me? Cannot you tell me what actually occurred on that night?'

'I—I can't!' she blurted forth. Then, suddenly recovering herself, she added: 'I don't know what you mean.'

Her attitude puzzled me.

Again I endeavoured to persuade her to relate what had occurred between them, and there being no one in the vicinity to see or overhear, I placed my hand tenderly upon her shapely shoulder.

'I know it is not just to him to hold back anything that took place on that fateful night, but—but I can't tell you!' she cried, bursting into a flood of tears. 'I—I prefer to remain here, alone and desolate, with the memory of my dead love, than—than to reveal my shame!'

I saw that her young heart was overburdened by grief. Yet what was the nature of the secret she would not divulge?

I argued with her for a full hour, but she refused to tell me anything. Indeed, her attitude became more puzzling. Something had occurred on that night, but the mystery of it was inscrutable.

I told her that I should return to Milan at four o'clock that afternoon to catch the through express from Nice to Vienna, for I intended at all hazards to solve the problem of my friend's disappearance.

'I hope you will, Mr Morrice,' was all she said as she placed her small hand in mine for a moment, then bowing, turned away and left me.

I had sent a telegram to London, and being compelled to await a reply did not leave Bologna till just before midnight. But as I stood on the platform awaiting the train I saw, to my great surprise, the Donna Stella herself. She was alone, wearing a long fur travelling-coat and toque to match, and had not seen me. She travelled by the same train to Milan as myself, and next evening I watched her descend from my train at the Südbahnhof at Vienna.

On alighting, while I still remained unseen in my wagon-lit, I saw that she was met by a short, dark-bearded man and a thin, rather angular woman in brown, with whom she had a hurried conversation. She was apparently annoyed at their presence, for as soon as possible she escaped into the fine carriage which her uncle, the Prince, had sent for her.

As I drove down the brightly lit Heugasse, to the Bristol, I could not put aside the thought that the man had used threats towards her. I had noticed the expression of fear upon her pale face, half hidden by her veil.

Yet she had deliberately concealed the truth from me, and this had aroused my suspicions.

I had kept on my sitting-room and bedroom at the hotel, and, as I entered, the first object that greeted my eyes was my missing friend's curious purchase—the Brass Butterfly. I had given up Jack's rooms, and his belongings had been transferred to mine. Taking up the curious object I gazed at it in wonder, as I had done several times. Somehow I entertained a fixed belief that its purchase was in some way connected with his disappearance. The police of Vienna had enquired of every antique dealer in the city, but the person who had sold it could not be found.

About two o'clock next day, while keeping patient watch upon the private entrance of the big house of His Excellency, the Foreign Minister in the Franzens Ring, not far from my hotel, I saw the dark-eyed girl, neat in a brown tailor-made gown, come forth, and walking as far as the corner of the Volksgarten, she entered a cab. Across the city I followed her to the Kronprinz Rudolf Strasse, where, turning down a side-street, close to the Danube, she entered a rather dingy house while her cab waited outside.

For perhaps three-quarters of an hour she remained there. When she emerged, she was accompanied by the same short, dark-bearded man who had met her at the station. He bowed to her as she drove off, but it was evident that there was a coolness between them.

The girl's sweet face was pale and haggard, and I saw that she had been greatly upset by what had transpired. Already my enquiries had revealed that the man's name was Karl von Weissenfeld, and that the woman was his sister Freda.

That evening I wrote Stella a note saying that I had seen her in Vienna, and asking her to meet me next morning in the Tirolehof, a small, quiet café in the Weihburg, where ladies

often go to drink milk. In response she rang me up on the telephone, saying that she would prefer to call at the hotel, as
someone might see her at the café.

Therefore at eleven next morning she was ushered into my
salon, but at sight of the Brass Butterfly she started, and drew
back almost in horror. I noticed that the mere sight of the
quaint object upset her.

'Why don't you put that horrible thing away, Mr Morrice—
away in some place of safety? Sell it, give it away, destroy it—
anything—only get rid of it!'

'Is sight of it so very painful to you, then?' I asked, greatly
surprised.

'I—I don't wish to see it,' she answered, pale and agitated. 'It
recalls—'

'Recalls what?' I asked, fixing my eyes upon hers as I took
the old perfume-burner and placed it within a small cabinet
near by.

'Ah!' she cried. 'No; do not ask me! You would not, if you
knew how much I suffer, because—because I can never tell you
the truth—because of my shame!'

'Then you know why Jack Devrill is missing, eh?' I said, still
looking straight into her splendid eyes. 'Answer me one question, signorina. Has that Brass Butterfly any connection with
his disappearance?'

She hesitated. I saw in her countenance fear and confusion.
At last she nodded in the affirmative.

'Then tell me the truth, signorina—the truth of what
occurred on the night of the ball?' I urged.

'I can't,' she cried. 'It shall never pass my lips!'

'And yet you are here in Vienna, because your secret is threatened with exposure,' I said very quietly, my gaze still upon her.

'*Dio!*' she gasped, starting. 'How do you know?'

'Your honour is at stake, Stella. Why not allow me to assist you against your enemies?' I asked. 'Why not tell the truth, and let me advise you? Let us combine to solve this mystery of poor Jack's disappearance. Surely you are convinced that I am your friend, as well as his?'

'If I told you, Mr Morrice, you would instantly become my enemy,' she said hoarsely, as, with a choking sob, she turned and left the room.

What did she mean? Her suggestion was that Jack's disappearance had been due to her—that she held a guilty knowledge of the truth.

That afternoon, while keeping vigilant watch upon the big house in the Franzens Ring, I saw, to my surprise, the man Von Weissenfeld call. He was admitted, and remained within for half an hour. Then he hailed a cab from the rank and drove to the Rheinisch Café, away in the Prater Strasse, where, at a table in a corner, two rather ill-dressed men awaited him. Seated where they could not observe me, I watched them holding a consultation in an undertone, and by it became convinced that some crooked business was afoot. I noticed, too, that one of the men took a pencil from his pocket, and when the waiter's back was turned he scribbled something upon the marble table-top.

At length the trio rose and, leaving the café, separated as soon as they were outside.

As soon as the waiter had gone up to the desk I left my seat, and crossing to get a newspaper which lay near, bent and discerned something very faintly written. It appeared to be 'Bristol 198–9'.

This surprised me, for the number of my room at the Bristol was 198, while 9 apparently stood for an appointment at nine o'clock.

What could it mean?

For two hours I remained there pretending to drink, until at last a tall, thin, shifty-eyed man with a reddish moustache entered, and seating himself at the table ordered a bock. Then, when the waiter had gone to obtain it, he bent and searched for the secret message. Having read it, he wetted his finger and quickly effaced it. Afterwards he drank his beer at a draught, paid, and went out.

Was it some appointment made at my rooms? I resolved to remain wary and vigilant.

Therefore, after eating my dinner that evening in the smart white-and-gold restaurant of the Bristol which you who know Vienna know so well, I ascended by the lift, and at about a quarter-past eight entered my sitting-room. Afterwards I switched off the light, and concealed myself behind the long green silk curtains which had been pulled across the windows.

Then I waited—waited so breathlessly that I could hear my own heart beat.

The clocks chimed nine. The waiter entered to make up my wood fire, and left. Then the telephone bell rang, and though I dearly wished to answer and ascertain who might wish to speak to me, I remained in my hiding-place.

Those moments of tension seemed hours. What was intended, I wondered, at nine o'clock?

About a quarter of an hour passed, as nearly as I could judge. My watch ticked with a noise like a threshing-machine.

Suddenly I heard the click of a latch, the door communicating with my bedroom slowly opened, and I saw, by the firelight, standing in the doorway the man with the red moustache. Behind him was Von Weissenfeld himself.

'It must be in here,' I heard the latter whisper in German. 'It certainly is not in the bedroom.'

'He may have sent it to London,' remarked his tall companion.

'No,' replied Von Weissenfeld. 'Stella told me today that it was here this morning. Look over there—in yonder cabinet.'

The man with the red moustache crept noiselessly across the room, opened the door of the cabinet, and with a quick exclamation of satisfaction drew forth the Brass Butterfly.

'Good!' cried Von Weissenfeld, in triumph. 'Then the secret will be ours after all!'

The fellow had transferred it to the small leather bag he carried in readiness, and was about to retire, when I sprang forth and covering him with my revolver, cried:

'I have watched you gentlemen! You are thieves, and I shall hand you over to the police!'

And at the same moment I placed my hand behind me, locking the door leading out upon the corridor.

Von Weissenfeld remained perfectly unperturbed. Indeed, I have never seen a man take discovery so calmly.

'I do not think, Herr Morrice, that it will be exactly wise to call the police,' he replied; 'for if so, I shall explain to them that you are a secret agent of the British Government!' and he stood before me in defiance.

I was wondering why, if the Butterfly were abstracted, the secret would be theirs. What secret?

'Make what statement you like, I intend to call the police,' I said determinedly, turning to find the button of the electric bell. By this action, however, I foolishly relaxed my vigilance for a second, and when I turned again, not having found the bell-push, I discovered that both men had drawn revolvers and were covering me.

'Touch that button and you're a dead man!' exclaimed Von Weissenfeld, determination upon his sinister face.

Instantly I saw myself in a dilemma, locked in that room with these two desperate thieves.

I demanded the return of the Brass Butterfly, but both men only laughed in my face.

'You and your friend Devrill played a clever game!' replied the dark-bearded fellow who had threatened Stella. 'But we have outwitted you. The secret is ours!'

At that moment, ere I could reply, there was a loud rapping at the door, and a woman's voice called my name.

It was Stella.

I replied that entry could be obtained through my bedroom, and next moment she burst in, accompanied by the manager of the hotel and three porters in uniform. At sight of them the intruders fell back.

'Ah, Mr Morrice!' she gasped breathlessly, 'I telephoned to you, but did not obtain a reply. I have been indiscreet. I have unwittingly told that man yonder something,' and she indicated Von Weissenfeld, 'and afterwards I felt certain he would come here tonight, in order to secure the Brass Butterfly—to kill you if necessary in order to obtain it.'

'The Butterfly is in the bag in that man's hand,' I said, pointing to it with my revolver. 'Come, give it to me!' I demanded, advancing towards him.

But the fellow thrust his weapon in my face in defiance.

'Josef!' said the hotel manager, 'just telephone for the police.' And the porter, thus addressed, crossed the room and obeyed.

Then the urbane manager induced both men to lay down their arms, an example which I followed, while ten minutes later a brigadier of police, accompanied by four agents, arrived. The bag was taken from Von Weissenfeld, the Butterfly handed back to me, and the two men, who had little to say, were arrested and afterwards conducted out.

Stella, left alone with me in the little salon, turned, and laying a trembling hand upon my arm, said in a low voice:

'Forgive me, Mr Morrice, for I ought to have revealed the whole truth to you before. I should have done so, but that man, Von Weissenfeld, forbade me, threatening to denounce me if I told you. What occurred between Jack and myself on that fateful night I can no longer conceal. We neither of us wished to dance, therefore I took him up to my uncle's smoking-room, which, you will perhaps remember, adjoins his private cabinet. Presently I left him while I went to my room to readjust my hair, which had become disarranged when waltzing with you. When I returned Jack was not there, but peeping through into my uncle's room I discovered him bending over the writing-table taking swift notes of two official-looking papers which he had taken from a drawer. At first he was unaware of my presence, but when, in horror, I charged him with espionage he admitted it, and then revealed to me his true position. I was bewildered. My first impulse was to go to my uncle and tell him, but he persuaded me to remain silent. It seems that an hour later Captain Devrill went to the central telegraph bureau, and dispatched a cipher message to London. The clerk, Von Weissenfeld, who took it over the counter, possessing some knowledge of the cipher used, made out a portion of it and, suppressing it, came to me next day to blackmail me. He was a complete stranger, but I have since ascertained that he is a secret agent of Germany, and hence, I suppose, knew something of your British cipher. He demanded that I should obtain from my uncle's writing-table the original of those two documents, and allow him to take a complete copy, otherwise he would denounce me for having given official information to my English lover. This I refused. Captain Devrill, before he left me, had entrusted me with a message for you.'

'For me!' I cried in surprise.

'Yes. He told me to tell you to unscrew the head from the Brass Butterfly and send to London what you found inside.'

With trembling hands I took up the antique brass ornament, and after some trouble found that the head really did unscrew, revealing a small cavity within.

There, concealed inside, was a piece of thin foreign note-paper covered with Jack's well-known handwriting. Glancing it through, I found, to my abject amazement, that it revealed Austria's immediate intention to defy Europe, by tearing up the Treaty of Berlin and to annex Bosnia and Herzegovina!

At first I could scarcely believe it credible. Yet previous knowledge of this amazing move which had actually received the Emperor's approval and signature, would place Downing Street in a position of defence. We would be forewarned, and consequently forearmed against being drawn into international complications!

The war-cloud had arisen, and we alone held knowledge of it! That brief telegram sent by Jack had been suppressed by Von Weissenfeld, hence our Chief was unaware of the success of our mission!

'But why did Jack disappear?' I exclaimed, speaking aloud to myself.

A postscript, addressed to me, however, explained it. 'I am going on to Sarajevo and Mostar, the capitals of Bosnia and Herzegovina,' he had scrawled. 'I shall endeavour to ascertain the feeling there, and so shall efface myself for a few weeks. There are reasons why I should leave Vienna hurriedly and disappear. Stella has discovered the truth concerning me, and others may perhaps know it. Tell the Chief I shall report myself among the deaths on 1st February. Be careful of this Brass Butterfly. I want it for my collection. Take care of yourself, old chap!'

'Ah!' I cried, 'I see quite clearly now. He feared to leave a note for me, and was compelled to catch the first train to Budapest. Therefore he hit upon the device of concealing the secret within the Brass Butterfly.'

'Why, today is the 2nd of February,' cried Stella, whose mind was greatly relieved by reading that postscript. 'Yesterday's *Times* would have arrived from London an hour ago.'

I rang and when the waiter brought the paper, we found beneath the 'In Memoriam' column:

DEVRILL.—In affectionate remembrance of Guy John Devrill, husband of Ann Devrill, who died at Belgrade, Serbia, on 1st February 1901.

At midnight, while the blackmailing telegraph clerk and his companion were helpless in the police cells charged with theft at the Hotel Bristol, I rolled myself up in the wagon-lit already on my way to London via Ostend, bearing with me the precious scrap of paper which contained news of that sudden political move which, a fortnight later, took the whole world by surprise.

Three weeks afterwards Jack turned up again at Whitehall as spruce and smiling as ever, but utterly amazed at the apprehension his sudden disappearance had caused.

Later he explained that Stella had hesitated to give me his message, feeling that by revealing what the Brass Butterfly contained she would further betray her uncle's secret. She had, of course, no idea why her lover had so suddenly vanished. Further, it seemed that Von Weissenfeld had feared to denounce us, lest it should have been discovered that he was a secret agent of Germany, while the Donna Stella had, on the day following my departure, returned to Bologna.

That early knowledge of Austria's hostile actions—which no doubt surprised you when you read them in the newspapers—enabled Great Britain to unite with Russia in preventing a bloody and disastrous war in Eastern Europe. Therefore the end surely justified the means.

Jack is retiring from the service, for he is to marry Stella. Whenever I go to smoke with him in his rooms in Half Moon Street, however, I cannot help recalling how that most vital and important secret of State reposed unsuspected for so many days within the head of that quaint object which now occupies such a prominent position upon the polished table against the wall—the Brass Butterfly.

MATCH POINT IN BERLIN

BY PATRICIA MCGERR

Selena sat in the restaurant at Templehof Airport and decided to treat herself to a fancy pastry as her last memento of Berlin. The delicately flaked dough with its rich topping of whipped cream seemed somehow to symbolize the life to which she was returning. In June she had graduated from Vassar—Class of '55. In October she was to be married. The summer's tour of Europe had been a final fling before settling down with the well-bred pleasant young man of whom her parents so thoroughly approved. They would slide into the social rounds of Washington's bright younger set whose major anxiety was the proper chilling of wines and the harmonious blending of dinner guests. Life with Raymond would be a good life, easy, comfortable, sheltered. And oh, so unexciting.

Stop it! She pulled herself back from the edge of melancholy. It's the letdown of being at journey's end. Plus perhaps a slight case of pre-bridal jitters. She checked her watch: 7:40. They had told her when she arrived at the airport for the New York flight that there would be about an hour's delay in takeoff. So there were twenty minutes left to drink her coffee, eat her pastry, and say goodbye to adventure.

Her eyes went to the entryway where a young man was just coming in. Tall, lean-faced, rangy, he wasn't exactly awkward, yet his arms and legs seemed to move on not quite the same wave length. So different from Raymond, she thought involuntarily, with his neat precise movements, all so coordinated and so easy to classify. The stranger's face was serious, even set; yet seeing the deep clefts in each cheek she felt she knew how he would look when he smiled.

I'd like to know him, she told herself, and then, as his eyes seemed about to meet hers, she turned sharply away, with a vague sense of disloyalty to Raymond. She fixed her gaze on the pastry tray, which was only a few tables away, studying it as if all her hope of heaven depended on a right choice between Schillerlocken and Buttercremetorte. So intense was her concentration that she didn't see the small shabby man until he was beside her.

"Excuse, fraulein." His English was accented but fluent. "You are American, no?" The question was rhetorical. He slid into the other chair as he spoke. It was only when he was seated that she became aware—from his short quick breaths, the whiteness of his knuckles as he gripped the table edge—that this was no ordinary encounter; not a pickup, not a beggar, not a peddler. This was a man under shattering tension, a man ripped apart by terror.

"Fraulein." He leaned closer to her. "I must speak quickly. It is necessary they see me talk with American. I have a list. It is important. It belongs to the Party. And it is trusted to me to deliver to our leader. But they say I am not loyal. They say I will sell this list to the Americans. This is not true. I sell nothing. All I have—" his clenched fist beat against his heart "—all I am is for the Party. But one accused me and they do not let me explain. They come in the night to kill me before I can sell the list. It is the names of those who work for the Party, those who are true and those who betray us. You understand?"

"No." Selena shook her head.

"No matter. It is necessary only they see me talk to you and see me give you something. So long they know I have the list, they think only to kill me before I can sell it. They give me no time to talk, to explain. But when they think I have deliver it already, they will not be in so much hurry to kill me. They will wish to have me alive, to take me to the leader and tell what I have done. Then I can give to him the list and prove that I always loyal. So please to put your hands on the table, fraulein."

Instinctively she obeyed and his hand moved with snake-like speed to place in hers a small oblong box.

"Now put it quickly away," he ordered.

"But I—this list—I don't—"

"Quick, fraulein, bitte!" His tone was so urgent that she transferred the box to her purse and snapped it shut.

"Now is all right." His tension went out in a long slow breath. "They have seen. They think it is too late to stop me selling. They bring me now to the leader."

"But what have you given me? I don't want—"

"Nothing, fraulein. I give you nothing. The box with the list is here." He slapped his palm on his vest pocket. "When I go to the leader I give it to him and he knows Stanovski is loyal. What I give you is a box of matches, a box of matches only. But they will think it is the box with the list for long enough to save my life."

"But if it's so important—to both sides—and they think I have it—" He was rising to leave. She clutched his sleeve. "I mean, if they'd kill you for it, they might—"

"To you, fraulein, they can do nothing. With me it is different. Something happens on a dark street to me, one of their own people. I disappear, who cares? But you are American. You are here in the light with many people. Very soon you walk on your plane and then you are back in your own country. No one can hurt you. Besides in fifteen minutes, maybe less, I give the list to the leader and everyone knows you have nothing. Only a box of matches, fraulein. When I am gone you will use them to light your cigarettes and when you strike them you will remember that you have saved a life." He stood, heels close together, and made a formal bow. "Wiedersehen, fraulein."

She watched him walk, almost jauntily, to the exit. Two men met him there and they exchanged greetings. To a casual observer it might have been a reunion of old friends. But there was something in the eyes of the other two, something in the way they arranged themselves on each side, so close that he might almost be lifted between them, that was like an icy finger on Selena's spine. The little man, she realized, was an enemy agent, carrying information valuable to the other side. Yet watching him, so small and helpless between his two allies, she felt glad that he still had his precious list, glad he would be able to prove himself "loyal."

The waitress approached and cut off her view of the door. She looked blankly at the tray that had seemed, only a few minutes ago, so enticing—the thick chocolate, the gooey pineapple, the vivid cherry-and-banana.

"No," she said vaguely. "No, thank you."

Somehow she had lost her taste for pastry.

Instead she poured her second cup of coffee, reached into

her purse for the cigarette that would, she hoped, be a sedative for her quaking nerves. Ordinarily the waiter would have been quick to light it, but now he was deep in argument with the pastry girl, presumably trying to explain why he had summoned her to serve cake to a lady who wanted none.

So Selena fumbled for and found her newest acquisition. It was, as the little man said, a matchbox, just like the other boxes she had been buying for ten pfennigs all through Germany. She pushed it open and reached for a match.

But there were none. The box was empty. No, not empty. Only empty of matches. The panel slid a little way and stuck. And what made it stick was a thin strip of microfilm. The list! Stanovski's list! In his fear and agitation he had reached into the wrong pocket, passed over the wrong box. Now he had nothing to give his leader, no way to prove his loyalty. He had delivered the list to an American. Who would ever believe he had done it by mistake? Or believing, make any differentiation between error and betrayal? The grim faces of his companions rose freezingly before her. And the leader, she thought, would be grimmer still. Unhappy little man.

But now—she pressed the box shut, thrust it back into her purse, and suddenly had sympathy only for herself. Now I have the list. I'm marked with having it. It was delivered to me with almost a blare of trumpets. And if those men were sent to take their colleague, dead or alive, to the leader, are there not others charged with—at any cost—recovering this filmstrip?

She glanced around the restaurant. It was full of people and none of them was looking at her. Yet it seemed—was it only her imagination?—that many eyes had dropped, turned aside, just before she looked their way. She stared through the distant glass wall into the dark. Out there was the runway down which her plane would come. She strained toward it, toward the safety of that cabin rising into the sky.

The American Embassy, she thought. No, that's in Bonn. In Berlin it's the United States Mission. They would want this list. I must take it to them. But to get up from the table, find a telephone, try to locate someone at the Mission and explain what she had—it was too much for her. You're safe here, Stanovski had said. Here there was light, there were people, and she couldn't bring herself to leave it for the unknown that might be just outside the door. I can't be a heroine, she decided. My best hope is to stay in this public place until my plane is announced. I'll turn the film over to the authorities when I'm safely in New York.

So Selena sat and sipped her coffee and planned to thrust herself into the very center of the group that would move through the exit to the field and onto the plane.

At last it came—the announcement for which she was waiting. "Achtung," and the loudspeaker went on in German of which she caught the names of Hamburg, London, and New York, so she knew it was her flight being reported. But as the announcement continued, a dismayed murmuring rose from the people who understood it. More delay, Selena realised, and wondered how she could get through another half hour or more with the matchbox hotter in her purse than if all its original contents had been ablaze.

"Attention," said the loudspeaker and she leaned forward to concentrate on the English translation. With each word her heart sank nearer to despair. Unfavorable weather conditions.

Flight canceled. No more planes would take off from Berlin that night.

Around her the murmurs were tinged with irritation, anger, disgust. But Selena felt only numbness, as if nightmare had taken hold and none of this could be real. There was no safe cabin to walk to, no plane to lift her high above danger. There was only darkness and fog and evil.

Around her people gathered up their wraps and bags, preparatory to returning to their homes and hotels for the night. These were people who would be inconvenienced, missing business appointments or social engagements, because of the canceled flight.

But I—Selena pressed her purse tightly against her stomach—I have no urgent appointments. An overnight delay will make no great difference. I have nothing to lose—nothing but my life.

A few people lingered to finish their coffee or dessert. Soon they would leave. The restaurant would close. The airport would be deserted. Then what would she do? Find a cab, go to a hotel, spend the night in Berlin. How far, she wondered almost with detachment, will I get? Will they wait till I'm well away from the airport or will it happen as soon as I step into the cab? When? And how?

If she could get to the airport authorities, tell them her story, perhaps they could protect her. But the reservation desk seemed an impossible distance away. Beyond the restaurant entry was a smaller room with tables and chairs in it and a place to check coats and hats. There might be people in this smaller room and there might not. Beyond the room was a broad expanse of corridor with doors opening from it that led—she didn't know where. To pass alone through all that empty space—no, it wasn't possible.

But there must be some way. Some help. All these people. I can't let them get away. If only I could speak a little of the language. Yet even if I did, how would I choose between a German who might befriend me and one of those who are waiting for me? How can I know whom to trust?

Once more she surveyed the restaurant. How, she asked herself, do you recognize an American? It's unfair, when everyone can tell I'm one, that I can't work it in reverse. In spy novels we give ourselves away by switching the fork from left hand to right after cutting our meat. But no one here is eating meat. And I've never heard of a distinctively American way of stirring coffee.

Behind her, at a table nearby but out of range of her vision, a voice was raised to ask the waiter for the check. A clipped British voice with an imperious accent that assumed everyone must speak his language. An Englishman! She twisted in her chair till she could see him. A comfortable, middle-aged, Colonel Blimp-type Englishman. So it's all right. I'll tell him what's happened, he'll take me to the American consul and—but no.

Before she moved she tried to compose her thoughts. Better not run to him with a wild tale of spies. He'll think I'm mad and it will give me completely away to whoever's watching. Instead I'll go calmly to his table and say that I'm alone in Berlin and need an escort back to my hotel. Then, once we're safely away from the airport, I'll tell him the story.

She rose and held tightly to the chair to steady herself till the weakness was gone from her knees. Then she turned. Colonel

Blimp was counting Deutchesmarks into the waiter's palm. But she hardly noticed the Englishman. For at the table behind and on the other side of hers was the young man she had seen earlier. And he was reading the European edition of the *New York Herald Tribune*. Reading the comics! So he was certainly an American. She wanted to shout the word aloud like a hymn. An American!

She almost ran to his table and the speech she had prepared for the Englishman tumbled from her lips.

"I'm an American and my flight home's been canceled. I'm all alone in Berlin and I—"

"Not any more you're not alone," he broke in cheerfully. "You're with Simon Mead now and there's not a better handler of damsels-in-distress on the whole continent than Simon Mead—especially when they're cuddly green-eyed damsels with raven distresses. Sit down, we'll have a little drink and then fly out under our own power."

She took the chair he pushed out, but she felt a stabbing disappointment. When he came in, she thought, he looked so sturdy, so competent, so able to cope with any emergency. Why must he turn out to be so hearty and clownish?

"I don't want a drink," she said. "I don't want to stay here."

"Sure you don't," he agreed. "Nothing deader than an airport when the fog closes in. The fun and games all went thataway. So we'll go after them. I'll tell you where we're going to start." His voice dropped to a confidential whisper as if they were already alone in a candlelit room. "The Zigeuner Keller of the Haus Wien. Know what that means? The gypsy cellar of the Vienna café. And it lives up to its name. Music that will break your heart and goulash that will ruin your stomach. Then from there—"

"I don't want to go to a night club," she protested. "I thought maybe you could take me to some place quiet and—"

"Ah!" His breath came out on a long rollicking note and ended in a whistle. "Know something, kiddo, I had you pegged all wrong. I was sitting here thinking you were my kind of dish, but I said to myself, uh-hunh, that's an icicle, go up and you'll get the old refrigerator door smack in your face. So I sit tight and you come to me. That's the kind of mistake I like to make."

"But I—"

"Don't worry, kiddo, if it's a quiet time you want, Mrs. Mead's boy Simon is for you. I've a nice cozy room, they'll send up some champagne, and we'll have ourselves a ball. Maybe you know my hotel?" Again his voice was caressingly low. "The Am Zoo. Funny name, huh? Means it's by the zoo. So you can listen to the lions roar outside and the wolf purr inside. How about that?" A grin creased his face, just the way she'd expected it would, but the sight gave her no satisfaction.

He rose and with a hand under her arm helped her from her seat and started toward the door. Unhappily, she let herself be drawn along, though only the memory of the perilous match-box in her bag kept her from pulling away from him. His conversation, as they threaded their way through the other tables, continued to be loud, jovial, suggestive. But as they passed the entry there was a sudden change. His grin faded, his voice dropped, and there was left no trace of heartiness.

"I'll take them off your hands now," he said briskly. "Our friend's matches."

"You—" She pulled her arm free. So he was one of Them. Or one of Us. In that instant she didn't care which. All that mattered was that he wanted the list and she wanted to get rid of it. The film had been forced on her. She had no responsibility for it, no ability to keep it safe. Let this man have it. And, more important, let everyone know he had it.

She half turned back into the restaurant. Look at me, she wanted to shout. Whoever you are, wherever you are, look at me. She fumbled in her purse, held the little box conspicuously aloft, and jabbed it toward her companion. See that. It was half a prayer. You must have seen that. I've given it away. I don't have it any more.

Her palm met his briefly as she pressed the box into it. He looked a little startled at the suddenness of her move but accepted the box and reached again for her arm.

"No," she said inanely. "I haven't finished my coffee. You go on. I'll stay here."

"Yeah?" He frowned, shrugged, was again the falsely jolly pickup. "Okay, this party was your idea, so you can call it off."

He swaggered away from her and disappeared into the room beyond. She walked back to her table, past Colonel Blimp who was stuffing his wallet into his pocket while he moved toward the exit. No need to speak to him now, she thought. I'm free of the list, free of danger. Yet the relief she should have felt was somehow missing.

The waiter hurried forward with her forgotten check. As she paid it and waited for her change, there was a commotion in the corridor, the sound of running feet and rising voices. No, she denied her fears. No, it's nothing to do with me. I can't go out there. Whatever's happening, I must stay here. But she ran, stumbling in her haste, to the door, past the checkroom, into the lobby where a chattering crowd had collected.

"What is it?" She seized the arm of the nearest man. "What's happened?"

He answered with a flow of German and she moved frantically on. Finally, near the outside exit, she found a woman who could speak English.

"The young man—the American—he has attack—a fainting fit. He falls and hits his head on the hard floor. But he has good luck that his friend is doctor. He takes him now to hospital."

"No!" Selena's agonized cry brought her only the curious glances of the nearest spectators. She pushed through them till she was at the door and could look out the glass into an open cab where Simon Mead's long form, limp now, his head dangling, was supported by a black-coated stranger.

"Stop!" She hurled herself past the obstructing bodies, out onto the sidewalk. "That's not a doctor. He has no friend."

But the cab was already moving and gaining speed. The crowd was breaking up, its moment of drama ended, returning to its own concerns.

"Stop them," she said again without much hope and no one paid any attention. The cab reached the first bend in the drive and would soon be out of sight.

I did this, she told herself, and the thought was a jagged wound. With my flaunting of the matchbox, my shoving it into his hand, I marked him for Them. Because I was afraid, I delivered him into their hands, sent him to—She couldn't finish the thought. She had to act.

Another car was at the curb, with an elderly couple inside giving instructions to a uniformed chauffeur. Selena pulled open the door, scrambled in, and almost onto the astonished owner's lap.

"Follow them!" The words took most of her remaining strength. "Follow that cab."

The man, his wife, and their driver stared at her in bewilderment. They say all Europe is corrupted with our American gangster movies, she thought bitterly, so that's a phrase they ought to understand. But they looked at her blankly, waiting courteously for some explanation of this wild American intrusion. And now the cab had vanished into the night. Only its license number, memorized without conscious volition, remained imprinted on her brain. Simon Mead was gone, he was helpless, and there was nothing more she could do.

But there must be. Her mind went back to those few minutes at his table. He had acted so well the part of brainless masher. He had talked a lot of nonsense. But he was there with a purpose, so his talk must have had a purpose too. He had told her his name, repeated it several times so she was sure to remember. And he had told her—what else? The name of his hotel.

Again his voice came back and the lowering of its tone took on new significance. He was giving her information that no one else should hear, telling her where help might be found. But she, filled with her own fears, had not listened carefully. Now she tried vainly to remember. It was her only hope. His only hope. She had to recall the hotel name. Something—yes, something about wolves and lions.

"Take me," she said to the driver, "to the zoo."

He looked past her at his employer. She turned to the old man.

"A hotel," she begged, "near the zoo." She tried various combinations. "Zoo Hotel? Hotel Zoo?"

"Hotel Am Zoo?" The woman supplied the name and Selena nodded gratefully.

"Hotel Am Zoo," she repeated. "Oh, hurry, please!"

The man and woman looked at her, spoke gently to each other. They could see she was in trouble, perhaps ill, certainly hysterical. Short of physical ejection, there was no way to get rid of her. That must have been their conclusion, for the man turned at last to the driver and spoke a command that contained the words "Hotel Am Zoo" and Selena relaxed a little as the car got under way.

But only for a moment. Where was Simon now? What were they doing to him? Would they take the list and let him go? Or would they—again her mind veered from inevitable conclusion. She sat on the edge of the seat and clenched her hands till the nails bit into the palms and tried to believe that it was not too late, that there was rescue for Simon at the end of her journey.

They rode through dark streets, narrow streets, and finally merged on the broad brightly lighted Kurfurstendamm. The car slowed, came to a halt, and she saw with glimmering hope the lettering of the Hotel Am Zoo marquee. She pressed the woman's hand, murmured a breathless "Thank you," and was out of the car before the chauffeur was halfway round to open the door. In an instant she was in the lobby, almost shouting Simon's name to the man behind the desk.

"Mr. Mead is not in," the clerk told her. "You wish to leave a message?"

"No, I—" She tried to calm herself, to collect her thoughts. "Is there someone here—someone who knows him—that I could talk to?"

"There is Mr. Mead's friend, Mr. Hartman. You wish to see Mr. Hartman?"

"Yes, please. And hurry."

With what seemed to her maddening slowness he turned to the switchboard operator. After minutes that might have been hours a stocky young man with a crew cut came toward her.

"Bill Hartman," he announced himself. "You looking for Simon? He ought to be back in a few minutes. If you'll come with me—"

"No, they've taken him away. He's in danger. He—"

"This way." Firmly he took her arm and propelled her to the short flight of stairs that led to the hotel's lounge.

"There's no time to lose," she insisted. "You've got to get help, find him—"

"Of course," he agreed soberly. "But first I have to know what's happened."

The lounge was a railed balcony that looked down on the lobby, its only occupant a man glancing impatiently at his watch. Bill Hartman took her to the back into a small glass-enclosed room to which treelike plants in large pots gave the appearance of a conservatory. He put her into a chair and took one close beside her.

"Now," he said, "tell me what you know and then I'll know what to do."

The authority of his voice and eyes gave her reassurance. She took a deep breath and told him quickly but fully about events at the airport from Stanovski's appearance at her table to Simon's unconscious exit. She held back only one detail—the flourish with which she had passed over the matchbox. To admit her cowardice, to expose to his friend her betrayal of Simon, was beyond her strength.

"You're sure," he said when she finished, "of the license number?"

"Very sure. Will it help?"

"It's good," he said, "that they started with the letters KB. That means a West Berlin registration and makes it less likely that Simon's been taken to the Soviet Zone." He was on his feet, looking down at her thoughtfully. "Now about you. I ought to take you some place where you'll be guarded, out of—"

"No!" she said vehemently. "Don't waste time. They know I gave him the matchbox. No one's interested in me now."

"I suppose that's true." He frowned, came to a decision. "All right, stay here. It should be as safe a place as any. Don't move from this spot until either Simon or I come back for you."

She watched through the glass of her shelter as he hurried down the steps, through the lobby, out of the hotel. Then she sank deeper into her chair and tried to tell herself that it was going to be all right. But there was no solace in her thoughts. Berlin was a huge city filled with hiding places and hostile forces. What could Bill Hartman or a dozen Bill Hartmans do to find one cab or one man in all that dark expanse? Again she was pervaded with a sense of guilt, a yearning to go back beyond that moment when her only desire had been to shift her danger to someone else.

Simon wanted the list, she told herself. He had asked for it. He was at the airport to get it. Yet she could not escape the belief that if she had made a less public presentation, had stayed beside him, the end might have been different. How he must despise me! I can't bear to face him. Yet she knew that to face him was the one thing above all else that she wanted. Only let him come back, she prayed. What he thinks of me doesn't matter. Only let him be safe.

A page came up the steps and gave a message to the man in the lounge. The man scowled, looked again at his watch, and rose to leave. Selena reached into her purse for cigarettes and matches. She put a cigarette between her lips, but the page was behind her, lighter extended, before she could take out a match. Inhaling deeply, she watched the man go down the stairs and the boy follow him.

She tried to make her mind a blank, to fill it only with the action in the lobby below, the movement of clerks and porters, the comings and goings of the guests. The next man to enter was, though she could not see his face, a familiar figure. The airport's Colonel Blimp. How different things might have been if she had spoken to him instead of Simon.

The Englishman stopped for a few moments at the desk, took a quick look around, and then, nimbly for a fat man, climbed the steps. He crossed the empty lounge and entered Selena's enclosure.

"My dear." He stood beside her chair, smiling down at her. "It's good to see you. I hoped that I might find you here."

"You—" She looked up at him, puzzled. "I don't think—"

"I told the porter that I had come to meet my niece and

102

described you. He sent me up here. Very convenient." He lowered himself into the next chair, pulled it closer to hers. "Now to business."

"I don't understand—"

"Please." He held up a plump well-manicured hand. "My time is too valuable to spend on games. You know why I am here. You have something that belongs to us. I have come for it. The matchbox, if you please."

"You're not an Englishman at all."

"It's a nationality," he said, "that I can counterfeit with great success. Very helpful in this business."

"Then you—you're a spy."

"We have the same trade, my dear. Only we work on opposite sides of the street. But I did not come to talk shop. Please return our property."

"I don't have it. I gave it away. You must have seen—"

"Yes, I saw. You made very certain that it was seen." He smiled at her and her cheeks flamed at the reminder. "You're a very clever girl. And you look so frivolous. Perhaps that is why you are valuable. Stanovski said that you were no one, that he had chosen you only because you were the first American he saw and he had given the list to you by mistake. At first we believed him. But no matter."

The shrug with which he dismissed Stanovski was casual, his smile still amiable. "He will bother us no longer with his lies. But you, my dear, I must admire your acting. You seemed so anxious to be rid of the matchbox, so uninterested in its contents. It was brilliant the way you used the young American as decoy to throw us off your trail and onto his."

The young American. Of all the man had said, Selena's attention focused on that one phrase.

"The young American—where is he? What have you done with him?"

"So now you grow concerned for your dupe." He chuckled. "A little late, is it not? But then you are like me, ruthless when there is a job to do. The innocent must be used and cast aside. If they suffer—well, it teaches them the length of our arm."

"What did you do to him?"

"An oafish tourist. They should not be allowed to wander loose and get in the way of serious business."

"But he—is he—"

"When I found that he was nothing, only a fool, I could not waste more time on him. We searched and found that you had given him a box of matches. Real matches. That was brilliant, my dear. But fortunately, though I was deceived, I was not entirely sleeping. I left someone at the airport to see where you went and I was able to follow. Now I will take the box— Stanovski's box. The one with our list."

He extended his palm confidently and Selena's hand closed tightly over the box she still held, the box she had not needed to open because the page had lighted her cigarette. It's not possible, she told herself. It can't be that the little man and I made the same mistake! He had intended to give her the wrong box but had handed her the right one. She, meaning to pass along the right one, had given Simon the wrong one. So now she still had the film, the list that both sides were so desperately seeking.

"You hesitate, my dear?" the fat man said cheerfully. "Surely you don't think I would come to you without a means of persuasion."

His hand dipped into his pocket and brought out a flat dark piece of wood. His thumb pressed a lever and three inches of narrow finely edged steel shot out. "If you have ideas about calling for help, let me tell you that it would take less than five seconds for this to slide between your ribs and into your heart. Then I would need only to summon a porter to help me carry my ailing niece to a taxi."

"You couldn't—you'd be stopped—you wouldn't—"

"Do you wish to put me to the test?" He switched the blade back into its case, held it close to her side. She shrank a little away, shaking her head without speaking. The cigarette dropped from her fingers. He picked it up and crushed it out neatly in the ashtray on the table in front of them.

"You're very wise," he approved. "Perhaps I'm bluffing, but in my trade you don't last long unless you're ready to follow through on a bluff. Now you will give me the matchbox."

"I—" Her throat was so dry she could hardly force the words. She closed her eyes and tried hard to swallow. This is what you wanted, she told herself. To be rid of the list, to be free of involvement. All you have to do is hand it to this man and it will all be over. Otherwise—

"I don't have it," she said.

"Don't be foolish." For the first time there was a snarl in his voice. "I know you have it. One way or another I'll get it from you. It will be pleasanter if you cooperate."

Yes, don't be foolish, one part of her was saying. You can't save the list, all you can do is get hurt. Give it to him before he has to use force. But her will was saying an irrevocable no. Maybe she was a coward, maybe at the airport she had been ready to save herself at any cost, but she wouldn't act like that again.

Simon Mead had risked his life for this list. She couldn't now surrender it tamely. When he came back—if he came back—at least she wouldn't have to tell him that she had given it up without a fight. The knife case was hard against her side. All right, she wanted to shout wildly. You have me, but you still don't have your list.

"Here." She thrust her purse at him. "Look for it yourself."

He opened the bag and dumped its contents on the table. She took advantage of this distraction to put the hand that was farthest from him, the one that held the matchbox, over the side of her chair till her fingers touched the soft earth of a potted plant. Showing no haste that might betray her, she dug a hole, buried the box, smoothed the surface of the soil.

"You see," she taunted as he probed the empty purse for hidden pockets. "I really don't have it."

"You don't have it in your bag," he amended. He swept the jumbled assortment back in and snapped the clasp. "It seems we must make a more thorough search than is proper for a hotel lounge. I must ask you to come with me."

He rose, fingering the knife with its unmistakable message. It's not too late, she thought. I could still give him the box and let him go away without me. Instead, she pressed hard against the chair, forcing herself to her feet. Only one thing seemed necessary—to get him away from the vicinity of the matchbox, away from this hotel before Simon came back to reveal his link with her.

They walked together down the steps. His hand was beneath her elbow, giving her chivalrous support. And the knife was in his hand.

"Your aunt will be pleased that I found you," he said as they passed the desk clerk. "She was afraid you might have left Berlin without seeing her again."

They walked out to the street. Kurfurstendamm was still as colorful, still as gay as the night before. Then she had been part of the gaiety. Now she looked hopelessly at the milling throng on the sidewalk, the groups sipping drinks at the outdoor café, and wondered if she would ever be one of them again. A cab was waiting at the curb. Her companion helped her into it, seated himself at her side, then banged the door.

"The young lady is not being sensible, Josef," he told the driver. "She wishes to make us work to recover our property. You know where to take her."

Josef nodded, swung the car away from the curb, out into the traffic.

"I am sensible," Selena protested. "If I had it I'd give it to you. I know you'd find it anyway. So it would be plain silly to try to keep it hidden."

"Extremely silly," he agreed. "But I encounter many silly people. However, if you wish to change your mind and give me the list it will improve your situation. You must realize that you are now quite beyond help."

"I do realize it. And if I had the box I would give it to you. But I swear I don't have it. I—I gave it away."

"Really? To whom?"

"I can't tell you that."

"Ah, but you can. I think you'll find that there's nothing you can't tell me, after we've had a little time together. I told you my time is valuable, but I'll spend as much of it with you as is necessary. As for you, you have plenty of time—the rest of your life, in fact. Tell me, Josef." He leaned forward. "You've had experience with Americans. How long will it take to persuade our young friend to tell us everything we want to know?"

"They're soft," the driver said contemptuously. "Ten minutes, if you're in a hurry."

"Ten minutes." He looked at her with lips thrust out, eyes narrowed speculatively. "Would you care to bet it takes longer?"

"No, I—" She pressed her hands together and strove for control. "I expect you can make me tell you everything I know. But I don't know anything. My orders were to go to the airport where a man would give me a matchbox. I was to take it to Hotel Am Zoo and someone would meet me in the lobby and take it from me. I did as I was told and that's all I know."

"And the person who took it from you. Who was that?"

"I don't know. I really don't." Draw them away from Bill Hartman, her mind warned, in case they learn that you spoke with him. "It was a woman. A woman I'd never seen before. She gave me the password and I gave her the matchbox. There was no need for me to know any more about her."

"Hmm." He rubbed his chin. "What do you think, Josef?"

"Could be," the driver answered. "They don't trust each other either."

"We'll see," the fat man said. "If you stick to your story through the next few hours, we may begin to believe it."

He patted her hand as if he were in fact an affectionate uncle and she felt a deep inner squirming. Ten minutes, Josef had said. Would it take less time or more? She had no standards by which to measure her own endurance and Josef was evidently an authority. She might as well take his word for it that in ten minutes she'd blurt out everything about Simon and Bill and send them back to the Am Zoo to dig the list out of the dirt. She'd been given a second chance to be brave and she was going to fail more dismally than the first.

"Please—" She took a deep breath, gathering all her strength. "I know I can't hold out against you. So—I'm ready now to tell you the truth."

"Ah." The man beside her let out his breath in a slow murmur and in the front seat Josef's husky chuckle showed satisfaction at finding an American even softer than his estimate.

"I—" She spoke slowly, choosing her words with care. "It's true what I told you, about them not giving me any more information than I needed and my not knowing who any of the other people are. But when they didn't know I was still there, I overheard something."

"Yes?" he prompted. "You overheard?"

"The woman I gave the matchbox to was to go to a café. She was to stay there from ten o'clock until eleven and a man would come, say the password, and take the box."

"The name of the café?"

"If I tell you, if I point out the woman to you, will you let me go?"

"Your life in exchange for our list? It may be a good bargain. We'll discuss it when the list is in my hand. Quickly now, the name of the café."

Quickly, her mind echoed, quickly, quickly. But she could not speed up her memory. Twice Simon had lowered his voice. Once it was to mention his hotel and she had found Bill Hartman there. Surely the other time was also significant, a signpost to a place of refuge. She *must* remember what he said.

"It's a place I never heard of." She turned to her companion for help. "A strange name—I think it was Hungarian. Or maybe Viennese. There was something—yes, about a cellar. And gypsy music."

"Gypsy cellar," he suggested. "The Zigeuner Keller of the Haus Wien?"

"Yes, oh, yes." She almost hugged him in her relief. "That's the place."

"All right, Josef, get us there fast." The car swerved round a corner, gathered speed. "We must be there before ten, before our list changes hands again. You've taken us on a roundabout chase, my dear. The Zigeuner Keller is almost next door to the Am Zoo."

"I didn't know that. I told you I only heard of it by accident."

"For your sake," he said softly, "I hope you've told me the truth. If this is a trick to gain time or to get yourself back among people, I'm afraid you'll deeply regret it. A crowded restaurant is no safer for you than this car. Remember how easily I took you out of the hotel? And people who waste my time have a very bad effect on my temper."

"It's not a waste of time," she breathed.

The car, once again on Berlin's main street, drew up in front of a vividly decorated building of gray stone.

"Wait for us, Josef," the fat man said, and helped Selena out of the car.

He kept her arm as they approached the building and continued to hold it as they descended the steep stairs that led to the dimly lit cellar.

"Simon Mead," she muttered as the uniformed doorman bowed them in.

"Eh?" The fat man frowned at her. "What's that?"

"He told me his name," she answered. "The American at the airport." They were beside the cashier. The headwaiter rushed forward with elaborate welcome. "I think it was—" she raised her voice a little "—Simon Mead."

The headwaiter, with sure professional instinct, greeted them in English, offered them a choice of tables in the three-quarter-filled dining room.

"We're meeting friends," the man told him. "We'll just walk round the room and see if they're here yet."

They made a slow tour of the cellar, inspecting the animated couples, the family groups. Passing a cluster of waiters near the raised platform on which the orchestra was temporarily at rest, she spoke again.

"Yes," she said, "I'm sure he called himself Simon Mead."

"Still worrying about that tourist," her escort grumbled. "Get your mind on finding the woman for me or you'll have more personal worries than that."

They completed the circuit. He selected a booth near the far wall from which the entrance was visible and sat down close beside her.

"So," he said, "we are ahead of her. That is good. Unless she is not coming. That will be most unfortunate for you."

"I only told you what I heard. The arrangement was for her

to be here. But that may have been changed. They may have made a different plan."

"Let us hope not, my dear," he said gently. "Let us both hope not."

The maroon-coated waiter was beside them with menus.

"Cognac," the fat man said. "And you, my dear? Do you wish to eat something?"

"Oh, no, nothing."

"Cognac," he repeated. "And mocha for the fraulein."

The waiter took the menus and scurried away.

"Now," he commanded, "keep close watch. We should not like to miss our friend."

Obediently she fixed her eyes on the entry. What now, she wondered desperately. How long will he wait before he knows that there is no woman, that I've lied to him? And when he knows it what will he do?

The waiter was back with their order. The fat man lifted the steaming pot, poured the thick strong coffee into her cup. Then he leaned back and took a connoisseur's sniff of his cognac. But he used only the hand farthest from her. The other remained on the bench, close to her side, so that she could always feel the curved wooden surface that masked the thin blade.

On the bandstand in front of her the orchestra finished their beers and went back to work. Violin, cello, piano, and marimba blended in a lilting tune with undertones of deep sadness. At the next table a boy reached for his girl's hand, gazed at her with misting eyes. Nearby, an exuberant diner waved his fork at the musicians in unison with the rhythm. From across the room came bursts of high-pitched laughter.

A short scream behind her brought her head around and she saw a spurt of flame. Fire! She felt a rising hope. If the restaurant's on fire there may be a chance for her to escape. But the blaze, she saw quickly, was only a row of skewered meat on which a waiter had poured brandy and touched a match. He waved it momentarily aloft before sliding it, still burning, onto a plate.

"Interesting," her companion murmured. "Have you ever seen a human torch, my dear?"

"No," she barely whispered.

"Much the same," he said. "Only of course we use gasoline. It's cheaper. Your woman should be getting here—if she's coming."

"Yes," she agreed. "She should be here soon."

She looked hopelessly round the room, from door to bandstand, past all the tables of happy people, to the back of the room where the white-capped heads of the chefs were visible above a screen. She looked at the screen, then looked away quickly, unable to believe her eyes. She glanced back and there was nothing there. Then a head bobbed up again—and it was Simon!

His eyes met hers, held them for an instant, and his hands, above the screen, moved apart in a sweeping gesture that told her to get away from the fat man, to free herself so that he could act.

There was no command she wanted to obey more. But there was no practical way to do it. Any movement on her part would only make her captor more alert. She wrenched her eyes from the kitchen, hoping that she had not given herself away. But her sudden tension could not miss being noticed.

"You have seen something?" the fat man said. "The woman—is she here?"

"I think so." Selena bit her lip, played for time. "Wait. Let me be sure."

Her eyes frenziedly roved the room, picked out a plump woman being seated by the waiter a few tables away. Her husband is probably checking his hat, Selena thought. But there may be time, just enough time, before he joins her.

"Yes, that's she." She pointed an unsteady finger. "In the red hat. She has the matchbox. But hurry. If she recognized me, sees us together, she may suspect—"

"Good." He slid his bulk from behind the table. "You've done well." He started away, turned back. "The password. What's the password?"

"Journey's end," she said.

He nodded soberly. In his trade, no doubt, he was used to odd phrases. He walked the few steps to the woman's table, looked down at her and spoke. She stared at him blankly and he spoke again, shouting to be heard above the music. The woman blinked, drew a little away in distaste, and he raised his voice just as the music came to a stop so that his repeated "Journey's end" boomed in the suddenly silent air.

"That's right." The answering voice was lower but audible to Selena's straining ears. "Your journey's ended, my friend."

Behind the fat man—close behind so that the weapon in the newcomer's pocket could press against the fat man's back—was Bill Hartman. And coming up to close the other flank was the cellist, incongruous in his yellow blouse and lavishly embroidered vest. The orchestra, a trio now, began a fresh tune, so

Selena could hear no more of what was said. But she saw the fat man shrug his submission and move with the other two toward the door in a tableau reminiscent of her last view of Stanovski at the airport. This time, though, she felt no chill.

She didn't watch them all the way out. Suddenly Simon was at her side, his voice soft but imperative.

"You're all right?" She turned and his eyes seemed to be memorizing every detail of her face.

"Yes, I—I'm all right." She felt, now that it was finished, an overwhelming limpness. Then, as she looked at him, her strength came flooding back and she repeated with honesty and fervor, "I'm perfectly all right. But your friends—there's a man outside in a cab—"

"We've got him," Simon answered. "Everything's under control now."

"But you—" She looked at him more closely, saw with a pang the red scar that ran from his hairline to an eyebrow. "You're hurt. What did they do to you?"

"It's nothing." He touched the mark lightly, laughed at her concern. "Don't worry about me. I'm indestructible. If you think this was a rough party, you should have been to the one in Hong Kong. Some day I'll tell you about it."

"Please do," she said eagerly, though her interest lay not in Hong Kong but in the promised contained in the words "some day."

"What happened tonight?" Selena went on. "How did you escape? At the airport you were unconscious. I saw them take you away." The memory came back with a vividness that made her shiver. "I thought they were going to kill you. And it was all my fault."

"Your fault?" His eyebrows lifted quizzically.

"I was so frightened." Fixing her eyes on her untouched coffee, she made her confession in a rush. "All I wanted was to save myself. That's why I made such a production of giving you the matchbox. I didn't think of the danger I was putting you into. The truth is, I didn't care. Not then, I didn't."

"As it turned out, that was the best job you could have done for me. Your big gesture made it easier for them to believe that you were using me, that I knew nothing about anything. By the time I came to, they'd finished their search and knew the list wasn't on me. All I had to do was go into my whiskey-brained playboy act till they were convinced they had the wrong man and you'd outsmarted them."

"And they let you go so easily?"

"An American tourist in the wrong hands can be a pretty hot potato. Let one disappear and it starts all kind of big wheels in motion. Headlines, diplomatic notes, high-level conferences, low-level investigations. Soviet-American relations are too delicate to put all that strain on them for no reason. And the way I looked to them, I was no reason. Worth nothing to either side. So they dumped me on the nearest street corner and got back to business."

"And you're—" She had to resist an impulse to run her fingers along the scar, to assure herself it was superficial. "You're all right?"

"Completely. The boy with the sandbag was careful to knock me out and nothing more. They wanted me in talking condition. But if you were worried about me, you can imagine how I've been kicking myself for throwing you to the wolves. Danger's my job. But you—"

He put his hand over hers, clasped it tightly as if to make sure she was really there. "Believe me, I thought you were well covered or I'd never have let them get the idea that you were the principal and I was your tool. The girl in the airport check-stand was working with us. Before they got to me, I had a chance to point you out and tell her to get you some guards. But you lit out too fast."

"I had to. When I saw them take you I had to try to find help."

"I know." He didn't release her hand. "I got a thousand-volt shock when I phoned the airport and found you'd gone out on the town alone. Then I got through to Hartman and he told me you'd showed up at the hotel. We raced back there and—" The pressure on her hand increased to the point of pain, but she didn't want it loosened. "The clerk said you'd left with your uncle. That's when I really panicked."

"But you found me," she soothed.

"Hartman kept his head," he continued. "He said since you got my message about the hotel, maybe the name of this place had stuck, too. We checked and found an American girl had been dropping my name and we knew we'd found you. Lord knows how you managed it, though. What witchcraft did you use to persuade our fat friend to go night-clubbing on the busiest night of his life?"

"I told him the list was—oh, I'd almost forgotten. The list is important, isn't it?"

"Worth everything you've been through for it," he said soberly. "The Reds have a cute trick of planting agents on our side and then expecting a double-cross. So they run periodic checks on their own team. This is the first time we've been able to run down one of their checkups. It will give us a valuable fix on who belongs to whom."

"Then we'd better get it." She started to rise. "It's in a pot at the Am Zoo."

"In a what? You'll have to decode that for me."

"I buried it," she said. "The list. In one of the hotel plants. We'd better hurry. If it's so important—"

"The list is all right." He held her down. "It's locked in a safe and photocopies are on their way to the proper places."

"How did you get it? Did you look in the pot?"

"You gave it to me." He studied her face as if he thought she might be feverish. "At the airport. Remember?"

"That was the wrong box. I made a mistake—"

"No, you didn't. The box you gave me had the microfilm in it. But I got rid of it fast. I hoped I'd get back to town whole. But that was something no one could guarantee. And the important thing was to save the list. So I passed it on to my friend at the checkstand before the other crowd closed in. I had another matchbox in my pocket. That's what made them think you'd done a sleight-of-hand. And I let them think it because I was sure that by then you were in a safe place. I didn't know I was getting myself off the hook by getting you on it."

"Then I didn't have the list? What I buried was just my own box of matches?"

"Let me get this straight." He spoke slowly, wonderingly. "Porky came to you and said you still had his film. And you believed him?"

"Yes, of course. I had another matchbox. I thought it must be the right one."

"But you refused to give it to him. Did he have a gun?"

"No, a—" Her voice shook a little at the recollection. "A knife."

"So you let him take you away. You thought you had what he wanted. You knew that all you had to do was hand him the matchbox and he'd leave you alone. Yet you deliberately hid the box and walked out with him. That took courage."

"No," she said. "I don't have any courage. I was scared to death. I've been scared from the beginning. I wasn't being brave. I just got mad."

"Maybe that's what makes heroes. Getting mad at the right time."

"But it was all for nothing," she said dolefully. "I could just as well have given him the box and saved all this fuss."

"Then you wouldn't have led Porky into our net. He and his friend Josef make a very good night's catch."

"They're important?"

"Not the biggest frogs in the puddle," he admitted. "But they make a fair splash. When they start talking—and a man like Porky, who's in it strictly for profit, doesn't need much encouragement to talk—I think we'll get some interesting revelations. You've been a valuable auxiliary, Selena."

"You—" She looked up, surprised. "You know my name?"

"Got it from the airline. You're the only passenger who didn't check in to change your reservation. It's the only concrete fact I have about you, but I intend to start a collection." His face lightened with the grin that would never lose its power to quicken her pulse. "For us, the journey's just beginning."

THE INTERROGATION OF THE PRISONER BUNG BY MISTER HAWKINS AND SERGEANT TREE

BY DAVID HUDDLE

The land in these provinces to the south of the capital city is so flat it would be possible to ride a bicycle from one end of this district to the other and to pedal only occasionally. The narrow highway passes over kilometers and kilometers of rice fields, laid out square and separated by slender green lines of grassy paddy-dikes and by irrigation ditches filled with bad water. The villages are far apart and small. Around them are clustered the little pockets of huts, the hamlets where the rice farmers live. The village that serves as the capital of this district is just large enough to have a proper marketplace. Close to the police compound, a detachment of Americans has set up its tents. These are lumps of new green canvas, and they sit on a concrete, French-built tennis court, long abandoned, not far from a large lily pond where women come in the morning to wash clothes and where policemen of the compound and their children come to swim and bathe in the late afternoon.

The door of a room to the rear of the District Police Headquarters is cracked for light and air. Outside noises—

chickens quarreling, children playing, the mellow grunting of the pigs owned by the police chief—these reach the ears of the three men inside the quiet room. The room is not a cell; it is more like a small bedroom.

The American is nervous and fully awake, but he forces himself to yawn and sips at his coffee. In front of him are his papers, the report forms, yellow notepaper, two pencils and a ball-point pen. Across the table from the American is Sergeant Tree, a young man who was noticed by the government of his country and taken from his studies to be sent to interpreter's school. Sergeant Tree has a pleasant and healthy face. He is accustomed to smiling, especially in the presence of Americans, who are, it happens, quite fond of him. Sergeant Tree knows that he has an admirable position working with Mister Hawkins; several of his unlucky classmates from interpreter's school serve nearer the shooting.

The prisoner, Bung, squats in the far corner of the room, his back at the intersection of the cool concrete walls. Bung is a large man for an Asian, but he is squatted down close to the floor. He was given a cigarette by the American when he was first brought into the room, but has finished smoking and holds the white filter inside his fist. Bung is not tied, nor restrained, but he squats perfectly still, his bare feet laid out flat and large on the floor. His hair, cut by his wife, is cropped short and uneven; his skin is dark, leathery, and there is a bruise below one of his shoulder blades. He looks only at the floor, and he wonders what he will do with the tip of the cigarette when the interrogation begins. He suspects that he ought to eat it now so that it will not be discovered later.

From the large barracks room on the other side of the building comes laughter and loud talking, the policemen changing shifts. Sergeant Tree smiles at these sounds. Some of the younger policemen are his friends. Hawkins, the American, does not seem to have heard. He is trying to think about sex, and he cannot concentrate.

"Ask the prisoner what his name is."

"What is your name?"

The prisoner reports that his name is Bung. The language startles Hawkins. He does not understand this language, except the first ten numbers of counting, and the words for yes and no. With Sergeant Tree helping him with the spelling, Hawkins enters the name into the proper blank.

"Ask the prisoner where he lives."

"Where do you live?"

The prisoner wails a string of language. He begins to weep as he speaks, and he goes on like this, swelling up the small room with the sound of his voice until he sees a warning twitch of the interpreter's hand. He stops immediately, as though corked. One of the police chief's pigs is snuffing over the ground just outside the door, rooting for scraps of food.

"What did he say?"

"He says that he is classed as a poor farmer, that he lives in the hamlet near where the soldiers found him, and that he has not seen his wife and his children for four days now and they do not know where he is.

"He says that he is not one of the enemy, although he has seen the enemy many times this year in his hamlet and in the village near his hamlet. He says that he was forced to give rice to the enemy on two different occasions, once at night, and another time during the day, and that he gave rice to the enemy only because they would have shot him if he had not.

"He says that he does not know the names of any of these men. He says that one of the men asked him to join them and to go with them, but that he told this man that he could not join them and go with them because he was poor and because his wife and his children would not be able to live without him to work for them to feed them. He says that the enemy men laughed at him when he said this but that they did not make him go with them when they left his house.

"He says that two days after the night the enemy came and took rice from him, the soldiers came to him in the field where he was working and made him walk with them for many kilometers, and made him climb into the back of a large truck, and put a cloth over his eyes, so that he did not see where the truck carried him and did not know where he was until he was put with some other people in a pen. He says that one of the soldiers hit him in the back with a weapon, because he was afraid at first to climb in the truck.

"He says that he does not have any money but that he has ten kilos of rice hidden beneath the floor of the kitchen of his house. He says that he would make us the gift of this rice if we would let him go back to his wife and children."

When he has finished his translation of the prisoner's speech, Sergeant Tree smiles at Mister Hawkins. Hawkins feels that he ought to write something down. He moves the pencil to a corner of the paper and writes down his service number, his Social Security number, the telephone number of his girlfriend in Silver

Spring, Maryland, and the amount of money he has saved in his allotment account.

"Ask the prisoner in what year he was born."

Hawkins has decided to end the interrogation of this prisoner as quickly as he can. If there is enough time left, he will find an excuse for Sergeant Tree and himself to drive the jeep into the village.

"In what year were you born?"

The prisoner tells the year of his birth.

"Ask the prisoner in what place he was born."

"In what place were you born?"

The prisoner tells the place of his birth.

"Ask the prisoner the name of his wife."

"What is the name of your wife?"

Bung gives the name of his wife.

"Ask the prisoner the names of his parents."

Bung tells the names.

"Ask the prisoner the names of his children."

"What are the names of your children?"

The American takes down these things on the form, painstakingly, with the help in the spelling from the interpreter, who has become bored with this. Hawkins fills all the blank spaces on the front of the form. Later, he will add his summary of the interrogation in the space provided on the back.

"Ask the prisoner the name of his hamlet chief."

"What is the name of your hamlet chief?"

The prisoner tells this name, and Hawkins takes it down on the notepaper. Hawkins has been trained to ask these questions.

If a prisoner gives one incorrect name, then all names given may be incorrect, all information secured unreliable.

Bung tells the name of his village chief, and the American takes it down. Hawkins tears off this sheet of notepaper and gives it to Sergeant Tree. He asks the interpreter to take this paper to the police chief to check if these are the correct names. Sergeant Tree does not like to deal with the police chief because the police chief treats him as if he were a farmer. But he leaves the room in the manner of someone engaged in important business. Bung continues to stare at the floor, afraid the American will kill him now that they are in this room together, alone.

Hawkins is again trying to think about sex. Again, he is finding it difficult to concentrate. He cannot choose between thinking about sex with his girlfriend Suzanne or with a plump girl who works in a souvenir shop in the village. The soft grunting of the pig outside catches his ear, and he finds that he is thinking of having sex with the pig. He takes another sheet of notepaper and begins calculating the number of days he has left to remain in Asia. The number turns out to be one hundred and thirty-three. This distresses him because the last time he calculated the number it was one hundred and thirty-five. He decides to think about food. He thinks of an omelet. He would like to have an omelet. His eyelids begin to close as he considers all the things that he likes to eat: an omelet, chocolate pie, macaroni, cookies, cheeseburgers, black-cherry Jell-O. He has a sudden vivid image of Suzanne's stomach, the path of downy hair to her navel. He stretches the muscles in his legs, and settles into concentration.

The clamor of chickens distracts him. Sergeant Tree has caused this noise by throwing a rock on his way back. The police chief refused to speak with him and required him to conduct his business with the secretary, whereas this secretary gloated over the indignity to Sergeant Tree, made many unnecessary delays and complications before letting the interpreter have a copy of the list of hamlet chiefs and village chiefs in the district.

Sergeant Tree enters the room, goes directly to the prisoner, with the toe of his boot kicks the prisoner on the shinbone. The boot hitting bone makes a wooden sound. Hawkins jerks up in his chair, but before he quite understands the situation, Sergeant Tree has shut the door to the small room and has kicked the prisoner's other shinbone. Bung responds with a grunt and holds his shins with his hands, drawing himself tighter into the corner.

"Wait!" The American stands up to restrain Sergeant Tree, but this is not necessary. Sergeant Tree has passed by the prisoner now and has gone to stand at his own side of the table. From underneath his uniform shirt he takes a rubber club, which he has borrowed from one of his policeman friends. He slaps the club on the table.

"He lies!" Sergeant Tree says this with as much evil as he can force into his voice.

"Hold on now. Let's check this out." Hawkins' sense of justice has been touched. He regards the prisoner as a clumsy, hulking sort, obviously not bright, but clearly honest.

"The police chief says that he lies!" Sergeant Tree announces. He shows Hawkins the paper listing the names of the hamlet chiefs and the village chiefs. With the door shut, the light in the small room is very dim, and it is difficult to locate the names on the list. Hawkins is disturbed by the darkness, is uncomfortable being so intimately together with two men. The breath of the interpreter has something sweetish to it. It occurs to Hawkins that now, since the prisoner has lied to them, there will probably not be enough time after the interrogation to take the jeep and drive into the village. This vexes him. He decides there must be something unhealthy in the diet of these people, something that causes this sweet-smelling breath.

Hawkins finds it almost impossible to read the columns of handwriting. He is confused. Sergeant Tree must show him the places on the list where the names of the prisoner's hamlet chief and village chief are written. They agree that the prisoner has given them incorrect names, though Hawkins is not certain of it. He wishes these things were less complicated, and he dreads what he knows must follow. He thinks regretfully of what could have happened if the prisoner had given the correct names: the interrogation would have ended quickly, the prisoner released; he and Sergeant Tree could have driven into the village in the jeep, wearing their sunglasses, with the cool wind whipping past them, dust billowing around the jeep, shoeshine boys shrieking, the girl in the souvenir shop going with him into the back room for a time.

Sergeant Tree goes to the prisoner, kneels on the floor beside him, and takes Bung's face between his hands. Tenderly, he draws the prisoner's head close to his own, and asks, almost absentmindedly, "Are you one of the enemy?"

"No."

All this strikes Hawkins as vaguely comic, someone saying, "I love you," in a high-school play.

Sergeant Tree spits in the face of the prisoner and then jams the prisoner's head back against the wall. Sergeant Tree stands up quickly, jerks the police club from the table, and starts beating the prisoner with random blows. Bung stays squatted down and covers his head with both arms. He makes a shrill noise.

Hawkins has seen this before in other interrogations. He listens closely, trying to hear everything: little shrieks coming from Sergeant Tree's throat, the chunking sound the rubber club makes. The American recognizes a kind of rightness in this, like the final slapping together of the bellies of a man and a woman.

Sergeant Tree stops. He stands, legs apart, facing the prisoner, his back to Hawkins. Bung keeps his squatting position, his arms crossed over his head.

The door scratches and opens just wide enough to let in a policeman friend of Sergeant Tree's, a skinny, rotten-toothed man, and a small boy. Hawkins has seen this boy and the policeman before. The two of them smile at the American and at Sergeant Tree, whom they admire for his education and for having achieved such an excellent position. Hawkins starts to send them back out, but decides to let them stay. He does not like to be discourteous to Asians.

Sergeant Tree acknowledges the presence of his friend and the boy. He sets the club on the table and removes his uniform shirt and the white T-shirt beneath it. His chest is powerful, but hairless. He catches Bung by the ears and jerks upward until the prisoner stands. Sergeant Tree is much shorter than the prisoner, and this he finds an advantage.

Hawkins notices that the muscles in Sergeant Tree's buttocks are clenched tight, and he admires this, finds it attractive. He has in his mind Suzanne. They are sitting on the back seat of the Oldsmobile. She has removed her stockings and garter belt, and now slides the panties down from her hips, down her legs, off one foot, keeping them dangling on one ankle, ready to be pulled up quickly in case someone comes to the car and catches them. Hawkins has perfect concentration. He sees her panties glow.

Sergeant Tree tears away the prisoner's shirt, first from one side of his chest and then the other. Bung's mouth sags open now, as though he were about to drool.

The boy clutches at the sleeve of the policeman to whisper in his ear. The policeman giggles. They hush when the American glances at them. Hawkins is furious because they have distracted him. He decides there is no privacy to be had in the entire country.

"Sergeant Tree, send these people out of here, please."

Sergeant Tree gives no sign that he has heard what Hawkins has said. He is poising himself to begin. Letting out a heaving grunt, Sergeant Tree chops with the police club, catching the prisoner directly in the center of the forehead. A flame begins in Bung's brain; he is conscious of a fire, blazing, blinding him. He feels the club touch him twice more, once at his ribs and once at his forearm.

"Are you the enemy?" Sergeant Tree screams.

The policeman and the boy squat beside each other near the door. They whisper to each other as they watch Sergeant Tree settle into the steady, methodical beating. Occasionally he pauses to ask the question again, but he gets no answer.

From a certain height, Hawkins can see that what is happening is profoundly sensible. He sees how deeply he loves these men in this room and how he respects them for the things they are doing. The knowledge rises in him, pushes to reveal itself. He stands up from his chair, virtually at attention.

A loud, hard smack swings the door wide open, and the room is filled with light. The Police Chief stands in the doorway, dressed in a crisp, white shirt, his rimless glasses sparkling. He is a fat man in the way that a good merchant might be fat—solid, confident, commanding. He stands with his hands on his hips, an authority in all matters. The policeman and the boy nod respectfully. The Police Chief walks to the table and picks up the list of hamlet chiefs and village chiefs. He examines this, and then he takes from his shirt pocket another paper, which is also a list of hamlet chiefs and village chiefs. He carries both lists to Sergeant Tree, who is kneeling in front of the prisoner. He shows Sergeant Tree the mistake he has made in getting a list that is out of date. He places the new list in Sergeant Tree's free hand, and then he takes the rubber club from Sergeant Tree's other hand and slaps it down across the top of Sergeant Tree's head. The Police Chief leaves the room, passing before the American, the policeman, the boy, not speaking or looking other than to the direction of the door.

It is late afternoon and the rain has come. Hawkins stands inside his tent, looking through the open flap. He likes to look out across the old tennis court at the big lily pond. He has been fond of water since he learned to water-ski. If the rain stops before dark, he will go out to join the policeman and the children who swim and bathe in the lily pond.

Walking out on the highway, with one kilometer still to go before he comes to the village, is Sergeant Tree. He is alone, the highway behind him and in front of him as far as he can see and nothing else around him but rain and the fields of wet, green rice. His head hurts and his arms are weary from the load of rice he carries. When he returned the prisoner to his hamlet, the man's wife made such a fuss Sergeant Tree had to shout at her to make her shut up, and then, while he was inside the prisoner's hut conducting the final arrangements for the prisoner's release, the rain came, and his policeman friends in the jeep left him to manage alone.

The ten kilos of rice he carries are heavy for him, and he would put his load down and leave it, except that he plans to sell the rice and add the money to what he has been saving to buy a .45 caliber pistol like the one Mister Hawkins carries at his hip. Sergeant Tree tries to think about how well-received he will be in California because he speaks the American language so well, and how it is likely that he will marry a rich American girl with very large breasts.

The prisoner Bung is delighted by the rain. It brought his children inside the hut, and the sounds of their fighting with each other make him happy. His wife came to him and touched him. The rice is cooking, and in a half hour his cousin will come, bringing with him the leader and two other members of Bung's squad. They will not be happy that half of their rice was taken by the interpreter to pay the American, but it will not be a disaster for them. The squad leader will be proud of Bung for gathering the information that he has—for he has memorized the guard routines at the police headquarters and at the old

French area where the Americans are staying. He has watched all the comings and goings at these places, and he has marked out in his mind the best avenues of approach, the best escape routes, and the best places to set up ambush. Also, he has discovered a way that they can lie in wait and kill the Police Chief. It will occur at the place where the Police Chief goes to urinate every morning at a certain time. Bung has much information inside his head, and he believes he will be praised by the members of his squad. It is even possible that he will receive a commendation from someone very high.

His wife brings the rifle that was hidden, and Bung sets to cleaning it, savoring the smell of the rice his wife places before him and of the American oil he uses on the weapon. He particularly enjoys taking the weapon apart and putting it together again. He is very fast at this.

THE ROCKING-HORSE SPY

BY TED ALLBEURY

As he sat on the bench in the Science Museum watching Robbie turn the handle of one of the glass-cased models, he wondered why his day with his son never seemed to come up to his expectations. The place was full of men like him— divorced fathers with 'access' on alternate Saturdays. There was no chance of being a real father. If he asked questions about what the boy did at home it was called 'snooping', trying to find out what she was up to. And there was just a very faint element of truth in the accusation. But if you couldn't be a real father, what could you be? A pal? What eight-year-old boy wants a forty-year-old pal? He thought about him so much when he wasn't with him but, somehow, it never seemed possible to express his feelings to the boy when they were together. Access Saturdays had become a grim, arid desert of frustration and disappointment. But the small boy seemed to take it in his stride.

Patterson smiled to himself as he watched his son, one stocking down to his ankle, his face intent on the wheels of the model turning slowly. A small girl walked up and stood watching with a man who was obviously her father. There was a second handle to the model, that worked a crane, and the girl reached out to turn it. Then to his dismay his son roughly pushed aside the little girl. 'Go away,' he shouted. 'This is mine.'

He hurried over. 'Apologise at once, Robbie. Say you're sorry.'

'I'm not sorry. This is my model.'

'Say you're sorry or we shall leave right away.'

The man with the small girl smiled diffidently. 'It's OK. It doesn't matter.'

Patterson caught his son's arm, swinging him round to face the girl.

'Say it. Say you're sorry.'

For a moment there was defiance then Robbie said reluctantly, 'I'm sorry.'

Patterson turned to the man. 'I'm sorry he was rude to your little girl.' He smiled. 'This is his favourite model but that's no excuse.'

The man smiled. 'I understand.' He shrugged. 'They are just children.'

'How about we all go to the café upstairs and have an ice-cream?'

'It's not necessary really.'

'I'd like to.'

The man shrugged and smiled. 'OK. Let's do that.'

As they sipped their coffees Patterson looked at the girl's father. His clothes were old-fashioned and his thin woollen tie had an untidy knot at his throat. His face was out of some Dickens novel. Large spaniel eyes, a full mouth; it was the face of a sad comedian.

When the children had eaten their ice-creams and were playing a guessing game, the two men were having a second coffee and Patterson said, 'Are you an "access father"?'

The man frowned. 'I don't understand. What is an "access father"?'

When Patterson had explained the other man said, 'My wife

was killed in a car accident six months ago. But, like you, I think I am a poor father.' He smiled diffidently. 'Plenty of love but no practical experience.'

'You speak very good English but you've got a slight accent.'

The man smiled. 'Part French, part Russian.'

'Have you lived here long?'

'Nearly a year now. I'm a freelance journalist. I write about electronics and computers.'

'Who do you write for?'

'Magazines, newspapers.' He smiled. 'Anyone who'll take my stuff.'

'Is that why you come to the Science Museum?'

The man laughed. 'No. We generally go to the Natural History Museum but it's closed today for building work.'

'Have you been to the zoo yet?'

'No.'

'How about we take the children to the zoo in two weeks' time? That's when I have Robbie again.'

'Why not? Where shall we meet?'

'Let's meet at the main entrance to the zoo at one o'clock.'

'Fine. I'll look forward to that.'

There was a message for him at the security desk. He was to go immediately to Logan's office.

He was surprised when he saw that it was not only Logan but also Chester and Harris who were waiting for him.

Logan pointed to a spare chair. 'Sit down, Patterson.'

When he was seated Logan leaned forward, his elbows on his desk. 'Where were you on Saturday?'

Patterson looked surprised. 'I had my son for the day.'

'Where did you go?'

'We had a snack at a hamburger place in Kensington. We went to a museum and then I took Robbie home.'

'Which museum was it?'

'The Science Museum.'

'Why did you go to that particular place?'

Patterson shrugged. 'What the hell is all this?'

'Why did you go there?'

'We go there frequently. My boy likes it there.'

'Tell us about Malik.'

'Who the hell is Malik?'

'You talked with him for nearly an hour in the museum café.'

Patterson explained what had happened and Logan said, 'What did you talk about?'

'His daughter and my son.' He shrugged. 'Just social chit-chat.'

'Didn't his name ring a bell?'

'I didn't ask his name. Why should I?'

'His name's Malik.'

'So what?'

'He's a Russian. Suspected KGB.'

'He told me he was a technical journalist.'

'He is. That's his cover. What else did he tell you?'

'Nothing. But we're taking our kids to the zoo in a couple of weeks' time.'

'Who suggested that?'

'I did.'

'Why?'

For the first time in the interview Patterson felt a surge of anger but he said quietly, 'Because it's very difficult, and rather lonely, trying to entertain a small child for a day and doing it as a foursome with someone with the same problem makes it easier.'

'Was that the only reason?'

'For God's sake. What other reason could there be?'

Before Logan could reply, Chester intervened. Chester was the senior of the three of them.

'What were your impressions of the Russian, Mr Patterson?' Chester spoke quietly and calmly and looked as if he would value Patterson's opinion.

'He seemed a quiet sort of man. Polite. Spoke excellent English. Obviously loved his little girl.'

'Did you like him? Did you feel you could get on with him on a friendly basis?'

'I didn't think about him that way. He was just a casual acquaintance.'

'I think your meeting could be very helpful.' Chester turned to look at Logan. 'I'd like to suggest that Mr Patterson takes over the surveillance of our friend Malik. He's in an ideal position to keep a close eye on him.'

Logan obviously resented the interference of his senior but agreed without protest to the new arrangement.

Patterson sat in his own office and read the details on Malik's file. He was forty-two. Born in Moscow. Languages at Moscow University and a science degree at Leningrad. Had served for six years at their embassy in Washington. Wife died in car collision in Kiev. One child. Father Russian. Mother French. There was little else beyond the surveillance reports.

The reports showed that he had contacted a wide span of high-technology industries in the UK and France. But it was no more than any conscientious science writer would have done. But equally, they were exactly the targets that a KGB man briefed to get secret technological information would have aimed at. A casual observer would never have seen Malik as an enemy agent but Patterson had been in MI5 too long to go by appearances. They didn't have to have their eyes close together or horns growing out of their foreheads. All too often they looked like your Uncle Charlie. And after all they probably *were* somebody's Uncle Charlie. Or Ivan, or Igor. Or in Malik's case, Grigor.

It was a fine day for the visit to the zoo and the children got on well together. Malik and Patterson sat on a bench in the sunshine as the children watched the sea-lions being fed. It was Malik who seemed to want to talk.

'My name's Malik. Grigor Malik. What's yours?'

'Patterson. Joe Patterson. Joe.'

'Shall I call you Joe?'

'Of course.'

'You live in London?'

'Yes. In Chelsea. A couple of rooms. And you?'

'I live in Chiswick.' He smiled. 'I've got a girl-friend. If things work out, maybe we get married. Maria likes her very much. It's her small house where we live. She's very kind to us both.' He nodded as he smiled. 'I like her very much.' He paused. 'I'd like you to meet her.'

'I'd like that, Grigor.'

'We could go back there for tea today. I told her I might

bring you and the boy back, if you agreed.'

'Fine. I'd enjoy that.'

'Do you have a new girl?'

'A few girl-friends but nothing serious.'

'You're not lonely, living alone?'

'Sometimes. But I get by.'

'How long have you been divorced?'

'Two years.'

'Is she married again?'

'Yes.'

The small terraced house in Chiswick was neat and well-kept. More or less what he had expected. But the girl-friend Kathie was a surprise. Irish, very pretty, lively and in her mid-twenties. And she obviously adored Malik and his daughter.

The children were playing in Maria's bedroom and the three of them sat around talking. Music and books.

She laughed, putting her hand on Malik's arm as she looked at Patterson. 'This one's a romantic. So it's Russian music and French novels. Proust and Flaubert with Rachmaninov and Tchaikovsky in the background.' She turned to look at Malik. 'Did you tell Joe about the rocking-horse?'

Malik smiled. 'No. You tell him.'

Kathie smiled. 'He's seen one of those beautifully carved rocking-horses and he's tempted to buy it for Maria. Do you know how much they cost? Three hundred pounds. It's crazy. He's going to borrow it from a bank.' She smiled at Malik affectionately. 'He's a big softy, this man.'

Malik smiled. 'That's what fathers are for, my love.'

The rocking-horse had been bought and the little girl's delight was obviously well-rewarding to Malik.

All through the summer Patterson had been a regular visitor to the house in Chiswick. Sometimes with Robbie and sometimes alone. In the early days he had found it disturbing to have such a close relationship with a man he was investigating. But as time went on and he was convinced that Malik was what he claimed to be—a journalist—he relaxed. He was aware that Malik had never revealed his nationality but there was no occasion when it would have been particularly appropriate. Robbie enjoyed his time with Maria and the Chiswick house had become almost a second home for both of them.

Patterson found it irksome when Logan congratulated him on his achieving such a close and useful relationship with a suspect. It made him aware of his own duplicity both to Logan and to Malik.

He had had long talks with the people who Malik had talked to at the various high-tech companies. There was no doubt that he was persuading people to give him information far beyond what was needed for genuine technical articles. And in some cases Malik had pretended to be a French national. But subterfuge and even deceit were not unknown to ordinary journalists. And he suggested this when submitting his reports to Logan. But Logan didn't share his views. For him Malik was a spy, an industrial spy maybe, but a spy all the same. Industrial espionage was part of the KGB's function in the West. They saved the Soviet Union billions of roubles in research costs, stealing from the NATO allies just as purposefully as they tried to undermine the fabric of Western society. Because of his views on Malik he was not consulted on the department's evaluation of his reports. He was shocked when he saw the piece on the front page of the *Evening Standard* which said that three suspect Russians were being held on suspicion of spying. There were grainy pictures of all of them and one was Malik. The *Daily Mail* the next day reported that the three Russians were being expelled.

In his time in MI5 he had been responsible for the prosecution and imprisonment of many people but they had been virtual strangers. Objects of suspicion, people to be kept under surveillance from a distance. He knew little about the effect of his work on their lives. And he had always been convinced of their guilt. But Malik was different. When he talked to Logan about his doubts, it was obvious that he wasn't interested. The Russians had thrown out two diplomats from the British Embassy in Moscow and London wanted to retaliate. They didn't necessarily have to be guilty of anything substantial. Malik was just an easy and available victim.

Some instinct made him want to see the girl, Kathie, and on the second day he'd gone out to Chiswick and walked to the road of old-fashioned Victorian houses. As he approached number sixteen he saw a small group of people and then he saw the 'For Sale' notice.

He made his way through the people to the front door. It was open and there was a handwritten notice saying that the sale of goods was on the following day. He walked into the front room. There were rows of domestic bits and pieces each marked with a price. Kettles, a toaster, a box of cutlery, crockery, plants in pots, a radio and TV and a record-player. Rolled up rugs and carpets, small items of furniture. And on a table by the far wall was the rocking-horse. He looked at the card pasted to the leather saddle. It said: 'Not for sale. Deliver to Gt. Ormond St. Children's Hospital.' As he turned away she was standing at the door looking at him. Her eyes red from weeping.

She said, 'They told me I could put up the prices because they were souvenirs of a spy.'

'But these are your things, Kathie, and why are you selling the house?'

'Was it you?'

'Was what me?'

'Somebody must have been watching him. They let me see him in the police cell for ten minutes. He said they knew everything about him. Me…' She shrugged helplessly.

'Did he say that he thought it was me?'

'No. He said you were his only friend.' She paused. 'They don't care about people, do they?'

'Did you know he was spying?'

She laughed harshly. 'If he was a spy then you and I are spies. What lies they all tell.'

'If there's anything I can do to help you, will you let me know?'

'You mean you can find me a nice, gentle man who loves me, and spends all his savings on a rocking-horse for a small girl?'

'I'll call in next week.'

'I won't be here.'

'Where will you be?'

'I've no idea. But I won't be here.' And he saw the tears on her cheeks as he turned to leave.

The Russians were on *News at Ten* that night. At Heathrow. Photographers and reporters running alongside them. As they stopped at the air-side gate a reporter thrust a microphone up to the first Russian. 'Have you got any comment, Mr Kreski?' The big, sour-faced Russian said, 'This country stinks.' A girl reporter spoke to Malik. He was carrying one case and Maria. The little girl was white faced, one arm around her father's neck. 'How do you feel about being expelled, Mr Malik?' For a moment Malik was silent and then he said, 'I am very sad to be leaving. I had good friends here. We liked it here, my daughter and I. People were very…'

Patterson leaned forward and switched off the TV.

Acknowledgments

The publishers are grateful for permission to include the following copyright material in this anthology:

"The Interrogation of the Prisoner Bung by Mister Hawkins and Sergeant Tree" by David Huddle, reprinted by permission of the author.

Cover image used by permission of Hulton Archive.

While every effort has been made to contact the copyright holders of material used in this collection, in the case of any accidental infringement, concerned parties are asked to contact the publishers.